Guarding

Kami

By Janean Worth

Chapter One

Gabe Mathews slouched down low in the seat of his car in front of the woman's house, waiting to catch a glimpse of her stalker. That is, if she even really had one.

His back was already protesting his hunched over position as he recalled again the conversation that he'd had with Stan just the day before. The conversation that had resulted in this uncomfortable stakeout. Stan had approached him right after the church service was over, when everyone was filtering out of the building, and had taken him aside to ask about the woman's problem.

"I'm telling you, Gabe, I think she's in real danger," Stan's voice had shaken with emotion.

"Stan, true stalkers are not that common. Are you sure your buddy at the police station has it right?" Gabe had asked, hoping that Stan was wrong.

"He said that she'd received a threatening note from someone who claimed to be watching her. He didn't go into details, because he couldn't share those, but he said he wished that the police could do more for her, other than just keep an eye on her house periodically. She lives in that big house of hers all alone. I'm worried about her."

The woman that Stan was so worried about was Kami Walker, a member of the congregation. Gabe had only met her a couple of times before, and at those times he'd gotten the feeling that she was quite a loner. She didn't mingle with the rest of the congregation much. She'd been polite to him when she'd talked to him, but her manner had been decidedly cool.

Still, despite her coolness, he'd felt obligated to at least check out what Stan had told him. Not only was it his Christian duty to look into the matter, but Gabe couldn't stomach the idea of a stalker harassing the woman. He'd seen the worst that could happen when a stalker took an interest in an unmarried woman, and he'd vowed that, if he had anything to do about it, that would not happen to another woman he knew.

So, Gabe now sat in his car near Kami Walker's house, in the middle of the night, feeling a bit like a stalker himself.

The shadows cast by the overhanging branches of the mature tree he'd parked under hid his plain blue sedan from view fairly well. The glow of the streetlight couldn't penetrate through the solid blackness of the thick shadows under the tree, and he was careful not to give his position away by using anything that would emit light. He didn't want her to see him and worry, and he didn't want to be spotted by the stalker, if she truly had one. He was as comfortable as he could make himself, which wasn't that comfortable, and he settled in for a long wait.

From his vantage point across the street, he could see her through the big bay window that faced out onto her massive front lawn.

In his opinion, the bay window afforded

entirely too much easy access for viewing her. He wondered why she didn't realize that. He wondered why Kami hadn't put up curtains or planted a large bush in front of the window to hide her from the view of the street.

Of course, he knew that the purpose of having an enormous bay window was for the view, so it would have been odd if she'd covered it up, but she was just so vulnerable behind that glass. So easily watched. So easily spied upon. So easily accessible to anyone who really, really wanted to get to her.

The thought of someone getting to her made him slightly angry. He wasn't surprised to realize that he felt protective of her already, even though he'd only been there a few hours and had only known her story for less than a day. It was well known in the Private Investigator business that it wasn't good to form a personal attachment to clients, but Gabe had always had a hard time with that rule. Even though Kami Walker wasn't a paying client, he'd already begun thinking of her as one of his responsibilities, and he *always* seemed to form a personal attachment to his clients in one way or another. He'd stopped fighting it long ago and now he believed that it might even be an element of what made him so good at what he did. The personal attachments drove him to success. They made him excel. Not for his own selfish benefit, but for theirs. He was good at what he did, but he was good because they needed him to be good.

Inside the house, Kami was moving around, tidying up before going to bed. An hour ago, she'd been gone from view for a while and had come back clothed in a simple black velour robe over a set of flannel pajamas covered in, if he was seeing it right

3

from this distance, a giant yellow happy face print. He had grinned when he'd been able to puzzle it out from a distance. Happy face pajamas! She was unusual, he'd give her that.

Kami had settled down on the sofa to read. A small lamp beside her on an elegantly simple end table was the only light in the room. The soft light enhanced her features, highlighting the soft curl of her hair as it fell over her brow and the gentle curve of her delicate jaw line.

He hadn't noticed before how attractive she was, but now, staring at her through the window, her vulnerable beauty nudged at him like a gentle wave on a sunset beach.

The minutes ticked by. To stay alert, he amused himself by counting the pages that she read as she turned them. He took stock of her surroundings every few seconds, cataloging the entry and exit points until he had them memorized. Soon, every single weakness exposed near the front of the house was cataloged into his memory until he had a mental blueprint of the area.

He'd have to come back in the daylight hours to see the rest of the house and grounds. If he left his vehicle now to go exploring what he couldn't see from his vantage point, he was afraid that he'd miss the action, if it ever came, and since action was his sole purpose for skulking out in front of her house like the stalker he was trying to catch a glimpse of, viewing the back vulnerabilities of her house would have to wait. He just hoped that the stalker would come at her from the front of the house. He was pretty sure a stalker would do just that, since the big bay window all but framed her for easy viewing.

His eyes drifted back to her face as she turned

another page. She was finally looking sleepy. Her head had slowly slipped to the side, until it rested against the sofa.

She dropped the book in her lap and yawned, then closed her eyes. Moments passed. Time seemed to slow for him.

When minutes passed with agonizing slowness and she didn't stir, he knew she had fallen asleep.

NO! He wanted to shout at her. How could she expose herself like that? How could she fall asleep in *front of the window?*

He wanted to shake her awake.

She should know better, shouldn't she? She had, after all, received a letter from someone who claimed to be watching her. Could she really be that naïve?

He suddenly felt an almost overwhelming need to protect her. He allowed his eyes to scan the darkness once again for any signs of her stalker.

Nothing. No movement. No whispers of sound. Nothing.

He struggled with the urge to leap from the car and charge up to her house and tell her that she should *not* be sleeping in front of the window. If he knocked, surely she'd be startled awake, and stop looking so completely defenseless and exposed behind the crystal clear glass.

How could she make herself such an easy target?

The stalker could be anywhere. With a good set of binoculars, the stalker would be able to watch her while she slept. For as long as he liked.

The thought drove Gabe crazy. He didn't want the stalker watching her while she slumbered, all innocent vulnerability in bright happy face pajamas. And if the stalker used binoculars and took advantage of the easy view, Gabe wouldn't even know it. He wouldn't be able to get a glimpse of her stalker.

She looked so childlike and defenseless, with the soft light shining on her face and the velour robe wrapped around her middle for warmth. He picked up his throwaway phone. The one he saved for when he needed to be anonymous. If he called her house, surely she'd wake up and then go off to bed?

It would be a waste of a clean phone, because once he used a throwaway phone, he never used it again on a different case. He didn't leave messy digital footprints like that. He knew better.

He tossed the phone back into the passenger seat. Too risky. The light from the phone would give him away if the stalker was near.

He fought down his protective emotions, realizing that, even for him, they were a little extreme. He shouldn't be feeling this way when he'd only just decided to look into her case yesterday. For pity's sake, if she saw him out here, she really would think *he* was the stalker.

She didn't know him very well. He doubted that she would even know who he was if he walked up to her door right now. And he didn't know her at all, except for a few chance meetings in church. Which was why he shouldn't be feeling so protective. Not yet. Just because her vulnerability pulled at his protective instincts so strongly didn't mean that she was like Jen. He couldn't help but draw the parallel between the two women, but he had to keep reminding himself that what had happened to Jen wasn't going to happen to the woman behind the bay window. He wouldn't let it. Not if it was humanly possible to prevent it.

He forced himself to remain still, slouched inside the blue sedan, muscles tensed in frustration, waiting for the stalker. He said a quick silent prayer for God's help in protecting Kami Walker, for His help in preventing another tragedy like what had happened to Jen.

Gabe felt torn, wishing both that the stalker would show up so that he could be observed, and that the stalker would stay away and not be able to watch Kami while she was so exposed.

His mind churned with the sheer flawed logic of her actions. Why, knowing that she had a stalker, had she so foolishly fallen asleep in front of the bay window?

It didn't make any sense to him.

Stan had mentioned in their conversation that his buddy on with the police had said how scared Kami had been when she'd come into the police station. Scared women, in his experience, did not fall asleep in front of a huge window with no curtains or concealment at midnight when they *knew* they had a stalker!

She should be hiding in her bed.

But the fact that she wasn't suddenly intrigued him. Maybe he had it wrong? Maybe she wasn't as naïve as she appeared? Perhaps she had been trying to get a glimpse of the stalker, just like he was, but she'd fallen asleep before he'd arrived?

Still, Gabe couldn't think of her actions as anything other than foolish. What if the stalker took it as an invitation?

Gabe slouched down in the seat even further, trying to ease the tightness from his cramped back and legs. He'd been sitting in the car watching her since darkness had fallen. And that had been hours ago. Earlier, he'd decided he wasn't leaving until she went off to bed. Now, he vowed to stay the rest of the night so he could watch over her. He just couldn't leave her there alone like that. Not when she might end up needing protection so very badly.

Chapter Two

Kami lay very still, heart pounding hard in her chest, pretending to be asleep. Was that him? There in the blue sedan across the street? Or was he somewhere else?

The blue sedan had shown up earlier in the evening. She didn't recognize it as belonging to the neighbor across the street, the neighbor whose house it had been parked in front of for hours now.

Through barely-open eyelids, struggling to keep her breathing even, she watched the car. She couldn't quite tell if the front seat was occupied, or if it was simply the headrest that made it appear as if there was someone behind the wheel.

Her neck was starting to ache from tension and she didn't know how much longer she could keep up the pretense of restful slumber without screaming.

And what was she doing anyway? She'd purposefully showcased herself in the lamplight on the sofa in front of the bay window. Hoping to catch a glimpse of the stalker that she now knew she had.

It was dangerous, what she was doing. It was foolhardy. But, at least it was action! The police had done nothing to help her when she'd gone to them last Thursday. Nothing! And now it was Monday night, and she'd barely slept since she'd received the note. The sleep deprivation was starting to make her doubt her own sanity and good judgment, which was probably why she'd thought it was a good idea to lie in front of the window, exposed like this in hopes of getting a look at the guy.

Tomorrow she was going to have to do something different. She couldn't keep living like this, feeling so afraid all of the time. But tonight she was going to do her best to be proactive and try to catch a glimpse of her stalker. Even if her heart pounded with fear and her neck ached with tension.

The police had said they'd send a car by every now and then, and she supposed they had, since she'd seen a police car drive through her quiet neighborhood on Saturday morning. But, the police had also said that they couldn't really do more than that until they had some real evidence of who the stalker might be or evidence of something he'd actually done. They'd kept the note that she had received from the stalker. They'd needed it for evidence. But the note was only a threat, and a threat didn't call for a protective detail, only for an investigation. As explicit as it had been, the police still hadn't done much to make her feel safe.

A chill raced up her spine, causing gooseflesh to raise up on her arms when she thought of the contents of the note. The stalker had been very specific. He was going to hurt her, but he was going to have a little fun with her first, and he was going to enjoy it. After he was done watching her, stalking her like an animal, then he planned to begin the real fun.

The thought made nausea rise up in her throat again.

She closed her eyes and prayed silently for

protection and strength, feeling desperation tangle with the fear in her chest.

The Lord was her only defense. She couldn't defend herself against he stalker at this very moment, because she didn't know who he was or where he was at, she could only pray that God would help her as she battled her fear.

She swallowed the dry lump in her throat and stared out into the darkness.

She couldn't see anything.

She sighed, suddenly tired of feeling like a china doll on display in a shop window. She'd had enough.

Reaching over, she switched off the light, got to her feet, stretched her sore neck and then strode through the heavy cloak of darkness to her bedroom. She may not be able to sleep, but she didn't have to make it easy for him to see her anymore. She could only take so much of that.

Maybe tomorrow she'd buy a dog. A nice, big, trained German Shepherd that would help her keep an eye out for the stalker. A big dog would be a good addition to the other security measures she'd been collecting since last Thursday. It was a good thing that money was no object, because in only four days, she'd had a security system installed, purchased a variety of small protection devices that she'd stashed at various locations around the house, and enrolled in a self-defense class. All of which had been very expensive. But she didn't feel bad about the money she'd spent. The money was part of the reason that she had acquired a stalker to begin with. At least she thought so anyway. Maybe it would be better if she went back to being dirt poor again, not rolling in money that she had never expected to have.

A woman could probably only have her picture in national newspapers, announcing her inherited wealth, so many times until she caught the eye of someone unsavory. And she'd shared headlines in many papers in the last year.

She sighed at the thought of all of the publicity. She'd really hated it all. She still wasn't sure why her grandfather had thought it was a good idea to make her the sole heiress to his wealth. She understood his reasoning, but it didn't change the fact that her aunt and uncle were both a closer relation to him than she was. They were his children, and she was only his grandchild. But, she supposed that since both her aunt and uncle had been estranged from her grandfather for more years than she could remember, and since she'd done her best to care for him in his last years, he'd thought it fitting to leave her his entire fortune.

If only he'd thought of the scandal that would ensue when he did so. If only he'd known how she'd be hounded by the press, and browbeaten by her aunt and uncle for months after his death, perhaps he'd have written his will differently.

She hadn't taken over his care for the money anyway. She'd done it because it was the right thing to do. The Christian thing to do. She'd done it to mend the rift he had created with his children so many years ago. The rift that had not been repaired before Kami's mother had died. Her mother had never spoken to her father again after their estrangement from one another, and he had not come to her funeral.

She sighed again in the darkness, silently willing herself not to think of her mother, her grandfather and his money, or the reason that she had

12

a stalker now. Trying to shake off the sleep that clouded her mind, and unwilling to turn on the light in case the stalker was out there somewhere with binoculars trained on her bedroom window, she tiptoed through the room.

Her feet sank into the thick, luxurious carpeting, making her steps silent in the big house.

Removing her robe, she tossed it over the antique French chair that had once belonged to her grandmother, but now sat next to her bed. Before climbing between her creamy white, vanilla-scented satin sheets, she carefully made her way to the nightstand and withdrew the small Taser that she'd stashed there.

Holding it in her hand like a safety line, she then went back to bed and snuggling down under the cream-colored sheets and the fluffy mound of her Egyptian cotton comforter. She almost felt safe with the Taser in her hand and the sheets pulled up to her chin. Almost.

It was at times like this when she believed her grandfather had been right about her lack of a husband. Grandfather had been opinionated and hardheaded and he'd insisted upon multiple occasions that a girl like her needed a husband to take care of her. She didn't particularly believe that was true at the time, but she hadn't argued with him, or taken the time to explain why she wasn't married. Revealing her inner pain over the betrayal of her former fiancé to her grandfather wouldn't have made her feel better anyway. The lonely hole in her heart had grown larger after her grandfather had gone to be with the Lord. She'd come to love the old codger dearly, and she missed him deeply.

A shudder coursed through her, and she could

feel the tears coming. Feeling so weak and helpless, alone in the dark, she let them come, knowing her grandfather had been right. If she'd had a husband, she wouldn't be facing this alone. And if she weren't an heiress, a millionaire three times over, then she wouldn't have a stalker at all. Being rich was as much of a curse as being poor. Even more so sometimes.

Chapter Three

"Hey, Gabe, you look terrible!"

Gabe stretched in his chair, trying to work the kink out of his back. The tight knot of muscles along his spine felt as if it might be permanently wedged there between his shoulder blades.

"Thanks, Jamie. You look terrific, as usual."

He leaned back in his over-sized office chair and stretched his arms over his head, only managing to loosen the kink slightly, then smiled at the ultra-slim brunette leaning casually against the door jamb of his office door.

Jamie was an odd one. She only helped him part time – when she felt like coming in to the office. When she did come into the office, she was part receptionist, part secretary, and part tech genius.

Gabe didn't mind her sporadic work appearances. He wasn't able to pay her much, and he appreciated the fact that she liked helping out more than she liked the paycheck. She'd told him once she'd work for free if he'd let her. He smiled at the recollection. Yes, Jamie was an odd one, but he was lucky to have her around to help.

She grinned back at him. "Thanks. Did you pull an all-nighter? I told Stan that you wouldn't be able to resist a damsel in distress after he confessed to telling you about Kami Walker's stalker. You could have called me for backup, though, you know? You need to get used to the idea that you're not in this alone anymore."

Gabe nodded, "I know."

"Or Stan. You could have called Stan. He'd have watched for the stalker and let you catch some shut-eye."

She straightened from her slouched position against the door jam and came around to the side of his desk to take a look at his computer screen.

"But Stan's got a wife and two kids, with a baby on the way. What would his wife think if I called him in the middle of the night to help with surveillance? He's not the private investigator. I am."

Jamie laughed, "He'd probably have been glad for some excitement if you'd called him."

It was Gabe's turn to laugh, "Surveillance is anything but exciting!"

Jamie shrugged, "You never know. He might find it exciting just because it is something new. I'm just suggesting that you didn't need to stay up all night, and that you need to remember that you are not all alone in the world anymore. You've got your church family to help you out when you need it now."

Jamie was right, he did need to remember that he wasn't alone anymore. He still had trouble asking people for help though, so it was going to be a while before he got used to it.

After Kami had left her living room and gone off to her bedroom somewhere in the house last night, he'd found that he'd been unable to leave her so unprotected. He'd spent the rest of the night

16

alternately staring at her house and staring into the darkness to find her stalker. He could have called for someone to help him, someone to relive him for a while so he could catch a nap, but the thought of asking for help was still so foreign to him that he hadn't even considered it. Being a loner was a hard habit to beat.

He shrugged his shoulders, both in response to Jamie's comment and in an effort to ease the responsibilities that sat so heavily upon his shoulders.

"You know, we've talked about these loner tendencies you have and the sudden attachments that you form for the victims. Cramming your six-foot-four bod into an unnatural position and going without sleep all night isn't gonna help her. You are not responsible for the problems of the world, Gabe. One of us could have helped you with the surveillance. And today you wouldn't be sleep deprived."

"You're right," Gabe admitted. "We've talked about it before, and I confess, it is hard for me to remember sometimes that I've got a family at church now. "

She gave him another playful grin and bumped his chair with her hip. "That's right, so move over and let me help."

"Ok. I admit it. I need your help. It's all yours," Gabe gestured to his computer and rolled the chair slightly away from the desk to give Jamie room as she bent over his keyboard. "Do your tech magic."

She threw him a wide grin over her shoulder, "You know I will. Already have, actually. I just want to share screens with your computer so that I can show you what I've come up with for starters."

Jamie tapped a few more keys on the keyboard, then stood. "There. You're hooked in to my computer now. I just wanted to show you the latest. Stan didn't happen to mention that Miss Kami had a past when he talked to you after the service on Sunday, did he?"

Gabe shook his head and leaned forward to take a look at the screen. Jamie had pulled up some headlines on CNN online.

Kami had a past?

He leaned closer and started reading at the same time that Jamie decided to fill him in, as if he wasn't getting to the pertinent stuff fast enough. Jamie was all about taking the shortest, most direct path.

"Seems her grandfather was a bit of a tycoon. He made his money in stocks. Smart, tough old guy if the papers have the right story. Anyway, he chose to make Kami his heiress instead of his own kids."

Gabe listened while perusing the pictures on the screen. The pictures must have been taken right after Kami's grandfather had died. She looked sad, and frightened by the crush of reporters standing around her in the photos. And she looked more than a little lost.

Jamie continued with her monologue, "Kami's parents and her aunt and uncle were estranged from their father, her grandfather. I haven't discovered why yet. It just says in the media coverage that none of his children had spoken to him in years. And there's more. Miss Kami has had a hard time of it."

Jamie leaned in to switch to a different online news source.

"Her parents were killed in a car accident before they could mend the rift. Kami grew up not knowing her grandfather, but after their death she decided to make peace with him. She made his last years better, or so the news reports.   And for that, he threw her to the wolves. I'm sure the guy thought he was helping her when he left her his entire fortune, but her aunt and uncle thought differently. So does the world, apparently. She's been dragged through the mud, Gabe."

Jamie switched webpages again and Gabe felt his jaw tighten.

On the screen, the headlines screamed that Kami was nothing but a money-grubber - out to take money from a senile old man.

Gabe didn't really know her, but from what he'd seen of her so far, he couldn't believe it was true. Could the slightly distant woman who kept to herself, but still attended church, be the money hungry leech that the media accused her of being? He didn't think so.

"There's more, but you look like you have enough to chew on for now. More later."

Gabe nodded, still staring at the screen. A large photo of Kami's face stared back at him. Her eyes were huge. They looked haunted and bereft, not greedy and self-serving.

"Got a few errands to run, I'll be back sometime. Call if you need me before then," Jamie announced as she sailed out of his office.

He nodded, still staring at Kami's frightened eyes on his computer monitor.

Chapter Four

Kami couldn't stand being alone in the house another minute. She felt trapped like a rat in a cage. Would it provide easier access for the stalker if she left the safety of her home? Or would he have better access to her if she stayed on familiar territory? She'd wondered about it all day as she'd paced back and forth across the marble tiles that lined the floor beside her indoor pool.

The pool room was attached to the back of the house, so she felt secluded and protected there, hidden away from prying eyes by the mirrored glass panes of the all-glass wall that looked out onto her massive back yard, and by the high privacy fence and tall evergreen trees that surrounded the yard. Still, even though she felt as if she were out of sight, being cooped up and anxious was driving her crazy. She stopped pacing and blew out a breath. Right or wrong, she'd had enough. She was going to get out of the house.

She pulled her cell phone out of her pocket, intending to call around to find out where she could buy a trained guard dog, but then put it back in her pocket. What if the stalker had somehow tapped her phone? She'd heard that a cell phone could be cloned, and that the person who cloned the phone could hear every conversation from the original cell phone, the same as if they'd made the call themselves. She wasn't sure if that was true, but she wasn't going to risk it. She stuffed her cell phone back in her pocket and left the poolroom in a hurry, before she could change her mind.

Grabbing her keys and her purse, she set the new security system, then went through the house to the attached garage and got into her old, beat up ten-year-old blue Mercury Sable. She'd had it forever, and she was sure that everyone was wondering why she kept it, with all the money her grandfather had left her she could have purchased a whole fleet of vehicles, but she was attached to the old thing. The old Mercury had been through a lot with her, and had always served her well. It still ran like a champ, so she had no reason to think of replacing it. She didn't care about how it looked.

The engine started right up, as usual, and she backed out of the large, empty six-car garage, punching the button to close the garage door when she was through it. She glanced around the area, then waited for the garage door to close completely before leaving the driveway. She wanted to make sure the stalker wouldn't be able to sneak in that way without tripping the alarm.

Having no idea where she was going, she began to drive. She realized that she could leave her house and drive around for days, and no one would care. In fact, no one would probably even notice – except for maybe the stalker.

It was her own fault. She'd isolated herself when she'd inherited her grandfather's money. Even the times she'd attended church in her area she'd felt alone and had ended up turning down what few invitations to functions that she'd garnered there. She was too afraid to be taken advantage of and hurt, and now she found herself totally alone in the world.

The money her grandfather had left her was turning out to be as much of a problem as poverty had been – even more in some areas of her life. She'd had more friends when she'd been dirt poor. Then she hadn't had to worry about what the people surrounding her were after. Then she'd known if they hung around her, it was because they wanted to – but she'd learned a few hard lessons since her grandfather had passed away, and none of them had been pleasant.

Cutting her musings short, she glanced in the mirror as she turned onto Central Street and headed for the closest strip mall. Last time she'd passed the strip mall, she'd thought she'd seen an ADT Security store there. Surely a security store would know somewhere that she could buy a trained dog for protection?

Turning into the busy traffic, she noticed that a blue sedan was following her. Her heartbeat picked up when she recognized it as the same car that had been parked across the street from her house last night.

She pressed on the accelerator hard and gunned the motor, picking up speed quickly. The Mercury might be old, but it still had some speed when she needed it. She sped down Central, thankful that the strip mall wasn't far away from the turn.

The dark blue sedan stayed with her as she dangerously crossed two lanes of traffic much too quickly in order to pull into the mall's driveway. She careened into the parking lot of the strip mall going a little faster than she should have been, tires squealing in protest. Finding a parking space was easy, and the car screeched to a halt as she maneuvered into the spot and stomped on the brakes. Before the car even stopped rocking from the fast stop, Kami was out of the door and headed for the ADT store. She didn't really have a plan, but perhaps the stalker wouldn't follow her inside. Stalkers didn't like to be seen harassing their victims in public, did they?

She ran through the door, breathing hard, and noticed out of the corner of her eye that the blue sedan had parked right next to her Mercury. Anxiety all but choked her. How foolish she'd been! How was she going to leave now, with the stalker parked right next to her car?

She quickly made her way to the tall shelves next to the door and hid around the backside so that she could see the blue sedan yet still remain hidden.

A man got out of the car and headed for the ADT store entrance. Her heart pounded harder. She groped in her purse for her Taser.

As he drew nearer, she couldn't help but notice that he didn't really look like stalker material. But he did look big and strong - strong enough to overpower her easily, whether or not she had a Taser. She shuddered and stepped completely behind the shelving as he entered the store.

She wished the store were larger. And she also wished that she'd have kept right on driving until she'd gotten to the police station. Now, she was trapped in the store with her stalker. Panic screamed along her nerve endings, making her hands shake and her thoughts jumble.

She closed her eyes and tried to calm her racing heart. She felt woozy from adrenaline.

"Kami?" a deep voice asked.

Her eyes popped open and she realized that he was right beside her. A startled shriek burst from her throat.

He held up his hands in a conciliatory manner, "Whoa! It's all right. Are you ok? I'm here to help you."

"Stay away from me," she warned, pulling the Taser from her purse.

"Is there a problem here?"

Kami turned to find a young teen boy standing behind her. His Adam's apple bobbed convulsively as he swallowed hard upon getting a good view of the man in front of her. The boy looked almost as afraid as she felt.

Kami felt like screaming again. This teenager was her only hope? The situation had just gone from bad to worse in that case. Not only was she herself in a bad position, she'd put the kid in harm's way too.

"No problem," the man said. "This is just a misunderstanding."

"I hope so, Pal, cuz I can call the cops," the boy threatened. The threat would have been more convincing if his voice hadn't cracked and gone girlishly high on the last syllable.

The man looked at her again, "Kami, my name is Gabe. Gabe Mathews. I'm a private investigator. Stan from the Church of Christ asked me to help you with your stalker problem. Do you remember Stan? He said you'd only been to the church a couple of times and that he'd heard from a friend of his at the police department that you had a stalker. I'm only here to help."

"I don't believe you. Your car was in front of my house last night. And you followed me here today."

"I'm sorry I frightened you. I didn't mean for you to see me following you today, but once you started driving like a crazy woman, I realized that I'd scared you. I just wanted to make it right so that you could relax a little. I'm not your stalker and I'm not here to hurt you."

Kami gave him her best glare. She didn't believe a word of it.

"Stalker?" the boy croaked, his Adam's apple bobbing again as he swallowed hard.

"Call Stan if you don't believe me, " the man suggested.

"I don't have his number," Kami grudgingly admitted.

"Have him look it up, then," the man gestured to the store clerk with one hand. "Or I can give it to you. I have it in my phone."

"Uh," Kami looked at the boy. "Would you mind?"

The kid shook his head.

"Is there anyone else in the store?" she asked hopefully.

The boy looked scared again, "Uh. Well… My boss will be back any minute. He just went to pick up some lunch. A while ago. So he'll be back any minute…"

The boy glanced at Gabe.

Kami knew what the teen was thinking. She didn't even have to ask. He was thinking the same thing she was. That they were alone in the store with a possible stalker.

The boy looked at her again, "If you'll come to the front counter, I'll look up your friend's phone number on the Net from my computer."

He took a couple of hesitant steps backward toward the front of the store, then leaned closer to her and asked quietly, "Do you know how to use that Taser, ma'am?"

Kami hadn't taken her eyes off Gabe, and she saw him smile.

It wasn't a vindictive smile, but rather one of genuine amusement. It lit up his face and made him seem attractive and perhaps even trustworthy. She tried glaring back at him to keep her suspicions active.

She couldn't trust him. She didn't know him. He really could be her stalker, although from what she'd heard, he wasn't behaving like a stalker would. He'd given his name in front of the boy and confronted her in a public place. Stalkers didn't do either of those things, did they?

She didn't know Stan well, and she had no idea why he would care if she had a stalker or not, but she began to hope that Gabe was telling the truth. If only because the smile that the man had given her made her long for something she was sadly lacking. Human companionship.

"I know how to use it. They showed me on Friday when I bought it," she assured the boy.

"Okay, well... then... The counter is over here." The teen wasted no more time making his way to the front counter, temporarily leaving her alone in the aisle with Gabe.

"You first," Kami gestured with the Taser to the front of the store. She didn't want the big man following behind her. At least if he was in front of her, she could see what he was doing.

"Fine by me," Gabe gave her another smile and walked quickly after the boy.

When Kami reached the front counter, she saw that the boy had wasted no time getting behind it and onto the computer. He was already bent toward the screen and had begun typing on the keyboard.

"Stan what?" he asked.

"Dramer. Stan Dramer," Kami told him.

The boy's fingers clicked quickly over the keys.

"There's only one listed," he said after a moment, smiling at Kami. He cranked the monitor of the computer around so she could see it. "There's his number right there. Do you have a cell phone?"

Kami nodded and pulled it from her pocket. She quickly dialed the number. Relief rushed through her when Stan's familiar voice answered.

"Stan? It's me. Kami. You know, from church?"

"Kami? Is everything ok? You sound frightened." Stan's voice was full of concern.

"Well, I don't know. There's this guy who'd been following me and he says you told him to. Says his name's Gabe and that he's a private investigator and that you asked him to help me?"

"Is he about six-foot-four with reddish-brown hair and blue eyes?"

Kami glanced at the big man next to her, looking him right in the eye for the first time. Blue eyes stared back at her from under dark auburn eyebrows.

"Yes," she answered.

"Then, yeah, that's Gabe. Sorry if he scared you. It's just that he's a private investigator and my buddy at the police station said that they really couldn't help you much when you came in. Gabe doesn't have to follow the same rules as they do, so I thought maybe he could help you."

Kami didn't know what to say. It was nice of Stan to care about what happened to her, but her system was still overloaded with the adrenaline from earlier and her hands still shook from the fright the man had given her. It would have been nice if Stan had given her some advanced warning.

"Is he there? Put the phone on speaker if you want and I'll talk to him. It will make you feel better."

Kami pressed the speaker button and held the phone out a little toward the big man.

"Stan?" Gabe spoke toward the phone.

"Yeah, Gabe. Seems like you gave Kami a scare? You should have told her what you were doing."

Gabe looked chagrined.

"I know. And I'm sorry," he directed the words at her instead of at the phone.

Kami could see that it was a heartfelt apology. She tried not to care, not quite over the scare yet, but a small part of her heart yearned for the promise of help and comfort in his voice.

"Kami?" Stan asked. "Are you ok now? I'll vouch for Gabe. I'm certain that he is the man standing there with you. I know his voice. You can trust him as much as you trust me."

It was Kami's turn to wince. She didn't really trust anyone, Stan included. How could she trust this stranger? Kami closed her eyes and said a quick silent prayer. *Please, Lord, guide me. Is he the help I was asking for?*

Opening her eyes, she sighed. "Yes, Stan, I am okay now. Thank you."

"Sure. What are friends for, Kami?" Stan

asked, causing Kami to wonder if he really considered himself to be her friend. She didn't know him that well and had only talked to him a few times at church. Stan's voice continued from the phone, "I hope to see you in church next Sunday? And if you need anything before then, just give me a call since you have my number now. My wife and I would be happy to help in any way that we can."

Kami's throat closed with emotion. The offer seemed genuine. It felt like forever since she'd had a true friend. She cleared the lump from her throat, "Thank you, Stan. I just might."

Stan hung up, and Kami returned the phone to her pocket.

An uncomfortable silence ensued, one in which Gabe stared at her, she stared at the floor, and the store clerk swallowed audibly several times.

"I really am sorry to have scared you so badly," Gabe broke the silence first. "I was only trying to help. I'm usually pretty good at my job."

Kami nodded, still at a loss for words.

The kid helped her out. "So, now that we know he's not a stalker, is there something I can help you with?"

He gave her a grin, as if what he'd said was terribly funny.

Kami returned his grin with a tepid one of her own, still more than a little impressed that he'd tried to help her, even knowing that the man beside her might have been a dangerous stalker.

"Yes, as a matter of fact. I came in to see if you have any idea where I could purchase a fully trained guard dog. Preferably a big one."

Chapter Five

Gabe couldn't help staring at Kami as she talked to the clerk about where she might find a guard dog. Standing close to her, he felt an almost magnetic pull. Something in her drew him like a moth to a flame. It wasn't her appearance, although that was very pleasant. She was a gorgeous woman up close. No, what drew him was something more. If he believed in love at first sight, and soul mates, and romantic myths like that, he might almost believe that was what he was feeling at the moment.

He couldn't remember ever feeling this way before, and he'd dated plenty of women. Something about Kami attracted him, and the reaction ran way deeper than a physical response.

He wasn't sure she accepted his apology for frightening her so badly. She really hadn't said anything in reply. He'd seen how badly her hands trembled earlier when she'd pulled the Taser from her purse, and the look on her delicate face had been pure panic.

He should have done a better job at tailing her. As soon as she'd started driving evasively, he'd known that she'd seen him. He chided himself. He usually *was* better at his job.

He realized he was still staring at her when she thanked the clerk and turned to leave. Without one word to him.

"Wait a minute, Kami. I'm coming with you."

He didn't give her any time to respond before taking her elbow in a firm grasp and leaving the store with her.

He thought he heard her mutter something under her breath about "high handed" and couldn't keep the grin from his face.

"I'm sorry if I seem that way to you, but now that you know who I am, there's no reason for us not to stay together. I'll drive you to take a look at the dogs. Would you like to take my car, or yours?"

She eyed his blue sedan, and he could tell she still didn't trust him.

"I'm sorry that you don't trust me yet, but believe me, I'm better than the alternative. You'll be safer with me than without me."

"I don't need your help," she said, looking exasperated and as though she didn't quite believe her own words.

"You know you do need help from someone, Kami, and I'm the only one here offering right at the moment, so you might as well accept it."

She sighed again and took a step away from him. She gathered herself to her full, diminutive height and looked him right in the eye. He had to admit, he liked that about her. For all that she seemed defenseless, she wasn't about to back down.

"Why are you doing this? You don't know me! Why would you offer to help? Is it the money? You know who I am, so you know I'm loaded. That's why you won't leave me alone, right? You want money."

Gabe felt the sting of outrage lance his pride. "No, that's not why."

He realized he'd raised his voice when she flinched a little and took another step back.

It was his turn to sigh.

He gentled his voice and continued, "I'm doing this because Stan asked me to. I'm doing it because it is what I do. I'm a private investigator. I help people. I'm doing it because you do need me, even if you won't admit that to yourself. I'm doing it for your own good, Kami."

Her eyes narrowed and she glared at him. "Very few people are that selfless, Gabe."

"Those who follow Christ are, Kami. Stan is from the same church we both go to. If we cannot help each other out in the body of Christ, then what will the world come to?"

He took a step and bridged the distance between them, then carefully took her hand in his. Looking into her face, he chose his words carefully. "Please, let me help you, Kami. No string attached. No money involved. Just help when you need it, from a fellow Christian. Okay?"

She gently pulled her hand from his as if his touch made her uncomfortable.

A moment passed as she stared back at him.

"Okay," she shrugged. "I'll give it a try. How much do you know?"

"Not much about the stalker. I was hoping you'd fill me in. The only thing Stan told me what that his police buddy thought you were in trouble, but the only thing they could do for you was to have a patrol car drive by your house frequently since the stalker hasn't done anything more than leave a note so far."

Kami nodded, "Yes, he left a note. Did Stan tell you what it said?"

Gabe shook his head, "No, his buddy couldn't give up that information."

Her fair cheeks pinkened and she looked embarrassed.

"I'm not sure I can repeat what it said to you. It was pretty explicit."

She turned away from him and opened the passenger door to his sedan.

"You can drive, okay? Do you know where this place is?"

He nodded, "Yes, I've heard of it."

She climbed inside and he shut the door after her, then made his way around to the driver's side of the vehicle and slid in next to her.

He couldn't help but notice that she scooted a little closer to the door, away from him. It made him wonder if she had something more against him than just trust issues.

The faint scent of her perfume wafted through the car as he started the ignition.

"You don't have to repeat word for word what the note said if it makes you uncomfortable. Just tell me if he made specific threats against you."

She turned her face away, cheeks pink again, and nodded as she stared out of the window. Her body tensed up in a defensive position, as if she was trying to make herself ready to face a threat.

Gabe sighed. The note must have really been bad if she reacted that way just talking about it.

"Why did you stay in front of my house last night?" she asked, still not looking at him.

"I was worried about you, and I wanted to see

if I could catch a glimpse of the stalker."

"Did you?" she turned to him, her green eyes dark with anxiety.

"No, I didn't. Why did you fall asleep in front of the window in the living room and make it easy for him to watch you if he was out there?" Gabe countered her question with one of his own.

A faint, self-deriding smile turned up the corners of her mouth. "I was trying to catch a glimpse of him too."

Chapter Six

The dog was enormous. A full-blooded German Shepherd with teeth like a saber-toothed tiger and a giant furry ruff covering his sloped shoulders. He looked menacing.

Kami liked him immediately. She paid the outrageous price they asked for him with out any quibbling at all. The trainer gave her a quick lesson on the commands that the dog knew and turned over the dog's leash when she gave him the check.

Gabe hadn't said anything at all during the transaction, but she could feel him staring at her. She wondered if he thought she was foolish to pay such an amount of money for a dog.

The dog behaved perfectly when she told him to get into the back seat of the sedan, and in just a short time they were headed back to the ADT office to retrieve her car.

Gabe was a surprise. He seemed unassuming and courteous, which was in complete contrast to his large size and rugged good looks. So far, he'd been the epitome of the helpful male. She couldn't fault his manners either. Still, she wondered at his motives. Despite the fact that he said he was helping her for purely altruistic reasons, in her past experience, people didn't usually work that way. No matter how badly she wanted to trust him and take him as this word, she just couldn't.

Her cell phone rang, startling her. She jumped and gasped, then gave a nervous laugh and smiled at Gabe in apology as she pulled the phone from her pocket.

"Hello?"

She felt the smile slide from her face and her insides clench up in fear at the sound of the derisive male laughter that came from the caller.

Gabe glanced at her, saw her expression, then mouthed for her to "put the phone on speaker".

She did, just in time for the caller to say, "You think either one of them can protect you? Nothing that the man or the dog can do will keep me away, Kami. You're mine. And when I come for you, nothing will stop me from having you."

Kami gasped.

Gabe reached over and took the phone from her grasp. She handed it over gladly.

"Who is this?" he asked the caller.

"Wouldn't you like to know, Mr. Gabe Mathews? Did you think I wouldn't see you last night? Did you think you could outsmart me, Mr. Private Investigator?"

The caller laughed again, and the sound of his derision sent a chill up Kami's spine. He knew who Gabe was? After only one night? And how had the man gotten her phone number?

"Kami is not yours," Gabe growled into the phone, and Kami saw a new side of the man. A protector. A strong capable protector.

For just a moment, she was glad he was there, until the caller continued with his taunts.

"You're just making it worse, Mr. Private Investigator. I did some digging. I know things about you, too. Not just Kami. I know things that she doesn't know. Things that she ought to know about you. You're not the saint you pretend to be, are you Mr. Private Investigator? Did you tell her about Jen?"

Gabe's face darkened and he punched the end call button on the phone and handed it back to her without a word.

"What's he talking about? What does he know? Who's Jen? How did he get my phone number?"

"Its nothing, Kami. Jen has nothing to do with you. Your situation has nothing to do with Jen. Just leave it alone. I'll handle it."

Gabe's lips compressed tightly. He looked so angry that Kami decided to follow his directive and just leave it alone. But she couldn't help wondering. Who was Jen? And what had the caller meant about the things she didn't know? And Gabe not being a saint?

Who should she believe? The stalker? Or Gabe? Who could she trust?

Her mind floundered in turmoil and her stomach responded and twisted with nausea. She closed her eyes and said a quick prayer: *please guide me, Lord.*

She leaned her head back against the seat and forced her roiling thoughts to calm. It would be okay. Everything would be okay. Somehow. She didn't know how, but somehow.

She felt the dog's nose nuzzle her cheek and opened her eyes. At least she had him. He seemed trustworthy enough right now.

"Good boy," she crooned to him and reached around to pat his huge head. "I think I'll call you True."

Chapter Seven

Gabe pulled into the enormous garage after Kami, parking beside her in the otherwise empty six-car garage.

She looked at him questioningly from the driver's seat of her old Mercury, then shrugged and pushed the automatic door button attached to her visor to close the garage door.

Gabe got out of his car and went to open her door for her.

"What are you doing?" she asked him suspiciously as she climbed from her Mercury.

He couldn't help but notice how she avoided stepping closer to him, even going so far as sidle sideways along the side of the car so she could allow the dog to exit the vehicle without having to move any closer to him. She'd remained silent the whole way back to retrieve her vehicle after the stalker had phoned her.

And he couldn't blame her. Not the way he'd snapped at her after the caller had mentioned Jen.

"I'm going to check the place out before I go, if that's ok with you? And, Kami, I strongly urge you not to stay here tonight. You can stay at my place, and I'll stay at my office. Or call Stan. Or go to a hotel. Something. Just don't stay here."

Her eyes widened a bit as she stared at him. "Do you really think that's necessary?"

He nodded, "I'm not trying to scare you. I just want you to be safe. And he's already gotten your phone number. He knows where you live. He knows about me. And about the dog. You have to ask yourself what else he knows about you. "

Her face paled noticeably as her eyes dilated slightly with apprehension. She shook her head. "I don't know. I don't know what he knows about me."

She looked so forlorn that he wanted to gather her into his arms and hold her. Protect her from the world. But he knew that she wouldn't let him. She didn't trust him yet. Instead, he gave her an awkward pat on the shoulder.

Her eyes moistened slightly at his gesture, and he thought for a moment that she might cry. But then she straightened her shoulders, shrugging away his hand as she did so.

"I'm fine," she told him, and he wondered if she was trying to convince herself more than she was trying to convince him. She stepped past him and hurried toward the door that adjoined the garage.

"Kami, you may think you're fine, and that you can manage this situation yourself, but you're under a lot of stress and this is not a normal situation. I really wish you'd consider staying elsewhere tonight."

"I said I'm fine," she shot back over her shoulder, her voice gaining a little strength.

She yanked the door open, flipped on the light switch and stomped into her house, then came to a dead stop.

He heard her gasp.

Quickly, he caught up with her and stepped around her body as she blocked the doorway, putting himself in front of her in case there was an immediate threat. He was impressed when the dog shot past them both to check things out.

The large, spacious kitchen that the garage opened into was an unbelievable mess. The place had not only been tossed, but the intruder had made sure to do as much damage as possible while inside her home. Every cupboard door was open, their contents dumped onto the floor. Shattered dishware covered the floor, mixed with the destroyed contents of the pantry and the refrigerator. Food from both were flung around on every surface, and what looked to be milk dripped off of the counter onto the floor. What must have once been shiny, pristine surfaces on the stainless steel appliances were now marred with giant dents, put there no doubt by the bent and damaged pots and pans, which also littered the floor. The glass from the double oven was broken out, as was the glass front of the stainless steel microwave.

Whoever had invaded her house had done a very thorough job of ruining her kitchen. Gabe muttered under his breath as he pulled his cell phone from his pocket and dialed 911.

Kami turned away from the mess, covering her face with her hands.

"This is Gabe Mathews," Gabe told the 911 operator after she answered on the first ring. "I'm here with Kami Walker. Her house has been broken into and her property has been vandalized. Please send someone over. Yes, your GPS has my correct location. Yes, I'll stay with her."

Gabe reached over and placed his palm on Kami's shoulders to offer support as he reported the crime. He felt her shoulder shudder against his hand.

"Thank you," Gabe ended the call and shoved his cell back in his pocket.

"I feel so alone," Kami whispered, sounding broken.

Gabe's heart twisted. He'd wanted to protect her from this – from the helpless feeling that stalkers engendered in their victims. He wrapped his other arm around her and gently drew her closer. She stiffened, but did not push him away; shocked enough by the damage to her home to allowed him to offer her comfort.

"He's going to get me, isn't he, Gabe? He's going to win," her voice sounded hoarse as she muttered into his shirt.

"No," he soothed. "No, he's not going to win, Kami. He's not going to win."

She shuddered again and Gabe winced. She was starting to lose it. And he couldn't blame her at all.

True growled.

And in that moment, Gabe realized that he'd made a mistake. He'd been distracted by Kami's reaction to her ruined kitchen. He hadn't checked to make sure they were alone in the house. He stiffened, slowly pushing Kami away and out of his embrace. Her tear-filled eyes met his gaze uncertainly.

"It's going to be okay," he said in a low whisper, for her ears only. "I'll be right back, you stay here with True."

He saw realization dawn on her expressive face. She'd realized what True's growl could have meant.

She shook her head at him, looking frightened. He gave her shoulders a squeeze, then pushed her closer to the wall and turned toward the kitchen doorway.

True growled again. The low sound was menacing. Gabe was suddenly glad that she'd bought the expensive guard dog. The animal had been aware of the danger when Gabe himself had gotten distracted by Kami's fear.

"I'm coming with you," Kami whispered as she sidled up to his side, her eyes huge.

"Let's not argue about this, Kami." Gabe took her hand in his and angled his body in front of her so that, from the doorway, he'd be the prime target for anyone who entered.

"Hello?" a masculine voice called from the front of the house. "Hello inside! This is the police. The door is open and I'm coming in."

"We're in the kitchen, officer," Gabe responded. *The front door was open?* It hadn't been open when they had arrived. He'd noticed that when they'd pulled into the garage.

Gabe's blood chilled as he realized what that meant. They *hadn't* been alone in the house. He silently berated himself. Searching the house and making sure Kami was safe should have been the first thing he had done! But he hadn't. He hadn't! True's warning may have just saved their lives.

"True, come," Kami called the dog back just as the officer entered the kitchen. The dog obeyed, but he directed a low growl toward the officer as the man stopped in the doorway and took in the damage to the room.

Kami's cell phone jingled.

"You expecting a call, Kami?" Gabe asked her.

"No," she shook her head. "That's my

43

ringtone for messages."

She let go of his hand and pulled the phone from her pocket, pressing a few buttons while she looked at the screen. Her face blanched white and he saw her sway as she closed her eyes and clenched her jaw.

"Kami?" he stepped closer, afraid she might faint.

Wordlessly, she handed the phone to him.

The picture on the screen was one of them embracing. Here in her kitchen. Just a few moments ago.

Chapter Eight

"I've found a bed and breakfast that will let me bring True and have him in the room with me," she said over her shoulder to Gabe as she gathered a few things to take for her stay.

"I would have kept him for you if you couldn't. I'm glad you decided to leave, I think it is the right choice."

Kami threw him a look over her shoulder, irritated by his words. "Do you think I'm stupid enough to stay here after what he did to my kitchen?"

"No, I wasn't implying anything. I'm just trying to be supportive." He shrugged his huge shoulders and then leaned against the doorjamb while she continued to cram clothes into her bag.

Kami suddenly realized that she'd become a little too comfortable with Gabe since this morning. She hadn't allowed a man into the house since her grandfather was alive, and here Gabe was leaning against the doorway to her bedroom. It felt odd to have him there. But, she realized that since the police had searched the entire house, including her bedroom, having Gabe standing in the doorway shouldn't make her feel any different than letting them invade the space. But it did. He made her feel safe.

"So, you really have no idea who might want to do this to you, Kami? The mess in the kitchen indicates that they're serious. Enraged, even. And definitely dangerous."

"No, like I told the police, I don't know who he could be. I don't know who would hate me so much, other than my aunt and uncle. As I explained to the police, they have been angry with me since my grandfather died and left me his entire estate." She stuffed three pairs of jeans into the bag and looked at him over her shoulder again. "You know, I didn't really want all of this."

She swung her hand around as if to indicate the huge house and the rich furnishings surrounding her.

"Why don't you give it to your aunt and uncle then, if you don't want it?"

Kami thought she heard suspicion in his voice. The same suspicion that she'd heard time and again since she'd become a millionaire.

"Can't. That was a stipulation of his will. I am to inherit the whole of his estate, but I am not allowed to give any portion of it to my aunt and uncle. Nor am I allowed to donate it all to charity. Believe me, I've thought of both."

Gabe snorted. "But why would he do that?"

Kami shrugged as she made her way to the closet and started pulling shirts off of their hangers. She shoved them in the bag, not caring that they would be horribly wrinkled later, and then bent to pick up a pair of shoes from the solid mahogany shoe rack at the bottom of the closet. She tossed them carelessly into the bag too.

"I really don't know. I tried to get him to tell me a couple of times why both my aunt and my uncle,

46

and my parents, were estranged from him. He wouldn't tell me the reason. And, since my parents are both gone, and my aunt and uncle aren't speaking to me, I guess I'll never know."

She brushed by him on her way to the bathroom to gather a few toiletries.

His voice followed her, "What could be so bad that you would never talk to your father again?"

Kami shrugged again, "I told you, I don't know. I'd give almost anything - forgive anything - if I could just talk to my dad again. I don't know what could have been so devastating that they never spoke again. My parents were loving. Even though we were very poor, we were happy. My grandfather was an embittered old man. When I first approached him, he was angry. He wouldn't talk to me for the longest time. But I kept trying."

She could feel Gabe's presence behind her as she entered the enormous bathroom. The soothing tones of peach and cream surrounded her, and the myriad of strategically placed mirrors allowed her to view him from almost any angle in the room.

"Why?" Gabe asked.

She met his eyes in a mirror. "I wanted to know him. I wanted to heal the rift, since my parents were gone and they couldn't do it themselves."

"You didn't care about his money, then?"

She smiled at the memory his question brought. "No, funny you should ask. At first, his money was the only stumbling block I had. I didn't mind his gruffness. Or the way he gave me the cold shoulder at first. I had expected that. What I did mind was that he lived so well, and had so much, and yet he'd let my parents live in a run-down trailer and barely scrape by each month. When I was a kid, we lived from paycheck to paycheck on my dad's meager salary for years, so my grandfather's vast wealth made me feel resentful. It was the one thing that almost made me want to stop trying to mend what had been broken."

She opened the recessed cabinet that held her toiletries and began hastily tossing them into another, smaller, travel bag.

"I understand better now," she told Gabe. "The money isolated him. Just as it has done to me. He knew that everyone wanted what he had, and so he shut himself off from the world to stay safe."

"Have you done that, Kami?"

She turned around, looking him in the eye. She felt like she was making a shameful confession. "Yes, I have. I have cut myself off from everything and everyone who could hurt me. But it didn't do any good, did it? Now I'm alone, and I have a stalker, and he is intent on hurting me. I didn't intend to isolate myself so thoroughly, and, until today, I hadn't even realized consciously that I was doing it."

She shook her head at her own naïve stupidity, then moved to brush past him so she could exit the luxurious bathroom.

He didn't budge an inch from his place in the doorway.

"It's not too late, Kami. And you aren't alone. I'm here to help."

Oh, how I wish I could believe that! Kami wanted more than anything to trust him. There was sincerity in his blue eyes, and although she wanted to open up, she couldn't forget the hard lessons her broken heart had learned. Logan's reprehensible actions had made her doubt all men. Especially to-good-to-be-true men like Gabe. In her limited experience, good-looking men did not come with big hearts and altruistic motives.

She smiled sadly, feeling the weight of distrust crushing her spirit even more. "I wish I could believe that, Gabe, but it's just not true. I am alone."

"You're wrong. You're never completely alone. Even if you don't accept my help for what it is, even if you don't trust me, Jesus is *always* there for you, Kami. If you cannot trust me yet, then trust Him. I'm helping you because of Him."

Emotion formed a painful lump in Kami's throat. That part was definitely true. Jesus *was* always there for her, and she was more comforted by that fact that anything else.

Chapter Nine

"I'm not going to argue with you about this Kami. It is the right thing to do," Gabe insisted as he helped her unload her large overnight bags from the beat-up Mercury. They were in front of the elegant castle bed and breakfast that she'd chosen, and of course, she was being obstinate again.

"But there's really no need for you to stay here, too," she assured him, trying to take the larger bag from him.

He didn't give it to her.

She sighed in frustration and blew her hair out of her face before she continued, "He doesn't know where I am. How could he when you led us on such a circuitous route here? And, was it really necessary to drive around for two hours before coming here?"

Her voice held a slight note of irritation as she held the door open to allow True's enormous bulk to exit the car, but Gabe knew she was just afraid. He'd come to realize that Kami had trouble accepting help - any help - even when she really needed it. And especially help offered by a man. He couldn't help but wonder what had made her so distrustful of men in general.

"Yes, it was necessary," he assured her. "If I

thought you'd go for it, I'd have insisted that we travel further, perhaps to Kansas City. Maybe even out of state. New York, or Dallas, even."

He closed the door to her Mercury and took her arm to get her attention. She was forced to look at him. "There's nothing that I won't do to help keep you safe, Kami. So, please, let me help you. And don't argue about the room anymore."

"Fine, but I'm paying. I insist." Her chin came up in that funny stubborn way that he was beginning to recognize.

Gabe shrugged, acting as if her footing the bill didn't bother him at all, when it really did sting. He was glad that she didn't know the extent of his own financial woes. If she'd known that he was almost bankrupt, then letting her foot the bill would sting even more. He was letting her have her way in this though, because he was unwilling to argue anymore with her. "Fine."

"Fine," she agreed, flipping her hair over her shoulder in a defiant gesture as she turned to walk up the cobblestone path to the entrance of the bed and breakfast.

He decided to change the subject, "I don't think that we should use our phones anymore while we are here. If he knows your number, he might just be good enough to get our GPS coordinates. Keep your phone turned off from now on, got it? And take the battery out. If you need to make a call, use this."

He handed her a new phone- a cheap, no-frills model he'd picked up to use for just such an occasion.

"It's a clean phone. Never used. And it isn't on a calling plan, so it will be harder for him to trace."

"Really? But, isn't that a bit extreme?"

"Trust me, Kami. This is what I do. Just trust me, for once. Use the phone."

He saw the dilemma in her anxious eyes. Why was it so hard for her to trust?

"Okay," she finally agreed, pocketing the cheap phone.

She didn't say anything else as she led the way into the bed and breakfast.

Gabe couldn't help but whistle softly as they entered the lobby. When she stayed somewhere, she stayed first-class. The place was more impressive than any other bed and breakfast he'd ever stayed in. The lobby floors were marble, in tasteful tones of gray and cream, shined to a mirror-bright gloss. Potted plants of various varieties dotted the enormous space, interspersed between tastefully grouped gold-and-cream tables and chairs. Cut flowers sat on every table, standing tall in crystal vases and filling the place with the scent of roses, hyacinth and eucalyptus.

"Nice, huh?" Kami grinned at him like a little girl in a candy shop. "There are some perks to my grandfather's money. I've never been to a place like this before."

Gabe grinned back, "Me either."

So much for his idea that she always traveled first-class. She wasn't at all what he expected sometimes.

At the counter, she gave her name, and Gabe didn't miss the clerk's speculative glance when he handed over a guest key to what was most likely their best suite.

"I'll need another suite and key for Mr. Mathews as well."

"That won't be a problem, Ms. Walker," the

clerk's lips twitched up in a disbelieving quirk. "Especially since you've rented the whole place for the foreseeable future."

Gabe coughed to cover his gasp of surprise. She'd rented the whole place? Indefinitely?

Kami flashed a smile in his direction, "I thought it would be easier that way. Fewer people around to watch out for. Besides, when I called earlier, they were unsure if having True around would upset the other guests. I figure, win-win. We get to stay here alone and True won't bother anyone."

Gabe smiled back. She was right, it would make things easier. And she was right on another count - her grandfather's money did come with perks. His smile faded when he realized that the same money was also probably the reason she had a stalker.

"You have The Royal Court room, Ms. Walker. And Mr. Walker will have the Scotland Yard room. Both on the second floor."

"Scotland Yard for you. Kind of appropriate, huh?" Kami asked, smiling. She finished checking them in and handed him his key. "I kind of like having the whole place to ourselves – complete with a staff to see to our every whim. Positively decadent!"

"Nice, thanks," He agreed. It was decadent. "This will certainly make my job easier." And it would. With only the two of them staying at the castle, anyone there other than the two of them would either be staff, or up to no good.

"I don't know why I've never thought to do something like this before," she frowned and shook her head as though something simple had escaped her. "But I'm willing to make the best of the situation now that I'm here."

She wiggled her eyebrows at him playfully,

and he was glad to see that she'd regained some of her spirit. He hadn't liked seeing her so scared and broken.

"You're having way too much fun with this," Gabe said, wiggling his eyebrows back at her.

She shrugged, "And why not? This money's got to be good for something. It sure has gotten me into a lot of trouble so far. And, after living so poor when I was a kid, sometimes these extravagances are kind of nice. Of course, they are just extravagances. Who really needs to live this way all of the time? But, luxury is really nice once in a while – especially when you really need it."

She gave him a look over her shoulder as she led True to the sturdy staircase made of polished wood that led to the second floor. "Don't get me started on how unfair it all is."

He shook his head at her, pasting a mock-innocent expression on his face, and rather enjoying this glimpse of her in a light-hearted mood, "I wouldn't dare."

She laughed as he followed her up the stairs and into the heart of the extraordinary bed and breakfast.

Chapter Ten

"Have you found anything, yet?" Gabe asked Jamie on the cell as he paced outside the hotel in the gorgeously manicured gardens provided for the guests. "I'm here with Kami at her bed and breakfast. No, no, of course it is not like that! I have my own room. Well, my own suite. You know why I can't tell you which bed and breakfast, right?"

"Of course," Jamie answered, and he thought he heard a smile in her voice, even through the phone. He knew she'd just been teasing when she'd implied he was staying in the bed and breakfast with Kami for his own personal reasons.

Hearing her fingers tapping keys on her multitude of keyboards at a very fast pace, he could imagine Jamie sitting in front of the bank of computers she kept in her office, keeping each machine busy searching for anything that would give them a lead on Kami's stalker.

"I'm sorry if it seems as if I've dumped this into your lap. I didn't intend to have to take her into hiding like this. Things are progressing faster than I thought they would. It is a good thing that Stan told me about this when he did."

"No problem, Dude. You know I love to help

when I can.   And I have plenty of time lately." She heaved a frustrated sigh.   "You know, it was much easier to come up with information when I didn't worry about breaking the law while I hacked."

Gabe couldn't help but laugh at the chagrin in her voice, "Yeah, I supposed it was. But, you can't tell me that you're not happier now that you've turned your life over to Him."

"No, absolutely not. I'm much happier and more content now. And if I thought I was able to open those virtual doors fast before when I was breaking the law, just think what He can do. I just have to remind myself that all things are possible through Him and remember to stop trying to do everything through my own power. It is a hard lesson to learn for a reformed hacker."

"I know, but you are right. All things are possible through Him," Gabe stopped pacing and leaned against a bench that sat along a quant little walkway near a group of rose bushes.

"Bingo!" Jamie shouted in his ear. "Yeah, all it took was a little faith, Dude! I got something.   I got in touch with ADT, the security company that installed Kami's brand new security system, and convinced them to turn over the digital footage from her security cameras. Of course, they had to check and recheck our credentials, but it looks like they've come through for us. I finally found something in the footage they sent. The guy who trashed her kitchen did a pretty good job of finding and disabling all of the cameras around her house before they could get a good shot of him. But he missed one, Gabe. We've got a decent face shot of him entering her kitchen. I'm going to clean it up digitally and see if Stan's friend at the police department would mind doing a search for us."

"Call me when you get more information? You'll have to use the number I just called you from. My regular cell will remain off until we know Kami is out of danger."

"Got it, Gabe. And yeah, I'll let you know as soon as I hear anything."

"Thanks, Jamie, I owe you one."

She snorted in his ear, "Ha, boss, you owe me more than one!"

She hung up on him, and he smiled and put the phone in his pocket. Jamie was invaluable. He had known it was a blessing when she'd joined him to help out in his office part time, and he'd been right. She was finding all the leads to help Kami. Now all he had to do was keep Kami safe until they figured out who her stalker was. And then find some way to catch him at his own game.

Chapter Eleven

Absence didn't always make the heart grow fonder.   Sometimes proximity did.   Or at least she thought so, Kami mused as she took True for a walk out in the gardens.   She was really starting to like Gabe, and it scared her.

Gabe wasn't like other men she'd known. Most men didn't have an unselfish bone in their bodies.   Logan certainly hadn't.   But Gabe seemed to be unselfish all the time.   Either Gabe wasn't like Logan at all, or he was a very good actor.

Now that she'd been forced to spend a little time with Gabe, she had a hard time imagining that he would be anything like Logan.   Logan had always been out to get what he could from life, even though she hadn't know it when she and Logan were dating.

Gabe didn't seem that way at all.   Logan had taken what she'd given, her companionship and love, and then berated her for not giving him more.   She'd tried to explain that the sort of intimacy that he wanted only came with marriage, and he'd grudgingly said he understood.   It had been months before she'd found out that he was secretly seeing not one, but two, other women on the side – and getting the intimacy that she had saved for marriage from them.

And when she'd asked him about them, he'd cruelly told her exactly what he thought of her. She'd been heart-broken to find that he thought her a prude, and that he had only continued to date her because her grandfather had been a millionaire several times over. He'd only been after money and sex, he'd told her.

Since then, she hadn't bothered to date anyone else.

"Would you like to have dinner with me, Kami?" Gabe's deep voice interrupted her thoughts and she jumped, just managing to stop a squeak from escaping her lips.

"Sure, sounds good," she agreed without thinking, trying to hide the fact that he'd managed to sneak up on her. She really should have been paying attention to her surroundings. What if he'd been the stalker?

He chucked, "Well, that was easy. Every other suggestion that I've made today has resulted in an argument."

She shrugged, "Food is different. We have to eat, don't we? And we are here together - might as well have dinner together."

"Do you want to eat here, or go somewhere?"

"Let's just eat here. I don't feel like being out in public. After everything that has happened today, I feel as if I have to keep looking over my shoulder. A nice quiet meal sounds perfect to me. Just you, me and True."

Gabe smiled at her. "How long has it been since you relaxed? Or slept? You look exhausted."

She smoothed her hair self-consciously with her free hand, and kept a hold on True's leash with the other. He was right. She was exhausted. And she probably looked awful.

She returned his smile wryly. It was a good thing he was helping her out of Christian charity, because it couldn't be her good looks he was sticking around for. "I haven't slept well since I received the note. And I haven't had a peaceful moment to relax since then either. Whenever there is a quiet moment, thoughts of what he said he was going to do to me in his note creep in, and I can't relax after thinking about that. Do I look that bad?"

"No, you don't look bad at all, Kami. You just look tired. After dinner, you can go lie down and sleep. I'll look out for you." His blue eyes were dark with compassion.

Kami felt her heart melt a little at the simple human kindness she saw in his gaze. He really *did* want to protect her. To help her. How long had it been since someone had wanted to help her for purely altruistic reasons? Not because they wanted her vast amount of money. Just help her because they were following Jesus' example?

Her eyes stung with emotion. She hoped he wasn't just a good actor, because she was starting to believe him. And he'd just offered her the one thing that she really, really needed. Someone to watch out for her. To keep her safe while she got some rest.

She'd bought True for that purpose, because she hadn't thought she had a chance of a person offering to help her. But Gabe had.

"Thank you, Gabe. That means more to me that you can possibly imagine."

He just nodded at her, looking at a loss for words. And in that moment, she realized that he would be an easy man to love. Unassuming, considerate, protective and a good Christian. All the things she'd always thought she wanted in a husband.

And here he was right in front of her.

She swallowed hard, and tried to put a leash on her rampant emotions. She couldn't fall for Gabe. She couldn't. She'd been through so much already, if he turned out to be a sham, then she knew she wouldn't be able to survive another broken heart.

And then there was also the problem of the stalker to deal with as well. Now wasn't a good time to start falling in love.

"You know, on second thought. Would you mind too much if I got a rain check for dinner? I think I need sleep right now much more than I need food." Calling herself every kind of coward, she felt bad for trying to wiggle out of their dinner arrangement. She really was bone-tired, so it wasn't a lie. Perhaps her extreme exhaustion would account for the closeness she was feeling toward Gabe now? At any rate, she didn't trust herself to have dinner with him without involving her heart. Not at the moment. Not when her defenses were down.

"I don't mind at all. I'll walk you to your room and you can get some rest. I need to catch up on a few things from the agency anyway."

Gabe looked at his watch, then glanced out the open door of his suite. From his strategic vantage point inside his suite, he could easily see down the short hallway that separated his suite from Kami's, and he had a clear view of the stairway as well.

No one had appeared in the hallway since Kami had gone to sleep.

And she'd been sleeping for eleven hours

already.   He stifled a yawn himself.   He hadn't allowed himself to fall into a deep sleep all night, but had instead just dozed periodically.   Several times, he'd wished he'd asked to share her suite and had just put a cot put behind the door. At least then he'd have been able to get a night's rest without worrying about someone getting into her room unnoticed. They were on the top floor of the castle, so there was no chance of access from the windows. That left only the stairway.

If it hadn't seemed so inappropriate, he might have had the courage to broach the subject to her. But she'd looked a little skittish when he'd walked her to her room, so he wasn't sure that she wouldn't have misconstrued his motives.

It was unlikely that whoever was stalking Kami would be able to find them here, anyway.   He had been careful. He'd made sure that they didn't have anyone following them before he'd even allowed Kami to head in the direction of the bed and breakfast.   They'd switched phones.   And he'd insisted that Kami use cash when paying for the rooms, so that her credit cards couldn't be traced. She was probably pretty safe here, but he had wanted to make certain that no one could get to her while she was resting.

The vulnerability he'd seen on her face last night had touched him deeply. He was now even more determined to protect her at all costs. She was exhausted and feeling alone, and too vulnerable to deal with this on her own, no matter how stubborn her protests were. She needed him. And he wasn't going to let her down.

Please, Lord, let me be enough to protect her. Help me to help her.

As if hearing his silent prayer, she opened her door a crack and stuck her head out. Looking cautiously first right, then left, like a small, shy turtle emerging from its shell, she checked the hallway for intruders. Her hair was tousled, sticking up around her head in a wild nimbus of curls, and she was wearing those odd happy face pajamas again.

She saw him through the open door, and smiled sheepishly, "I didn't mean to sleep so long!"

"You must have needed the rest," He stood up from the chair that he'd placed by his open door and stretched the kinks from his back, then crossed to the small table in his suite and grabbed the apple and orange that he'd ordered for her last night. He joined her in the hallway and handed the fruit to her. "I ordered these from the staff last night. I wasn't sure when you'd wake up, but I was pretty sure you'd be hungry since you skipped supper."

"Thank you, Gabe," her eyes softened as she took the fruit from him, something gentle and unguarded flickering across her expression. "I am hungry."

Suddenly, she seemed shy about looking him in the eye. And he thought he saw a blush tinting her cheeks.

"It's only fruit," he teased, liking the way that her cheeks pinkened even more.

She grinned a little, then immediately changed the subject.

"Would you mind taking True out for me?" Turning, she pushed her suite door open wider so that the dog could come out into the hallway. The large shepherd looked out of place in the posh surroundings of the bed and breakfast.

"No, I don't mind at all," he told her.

63

"I'll get his leash then," she disappeared into the suite, quickly reappearing with the leash. "Here you go. And thanks. For the fruit. For taking True out. And for letting me sleep so long. You didn't stay up all night, did you?"

Gabe shrugged, feeling uncomfortable with so much gratitude. He'd only done what any decent human being would have done.

"You did, didn't you? Well, I'll try to return the favor today, and guard the door so you can get some rest, okay?"

"Sure," he grinned at her, amused by the thought of her turning the tables and guarding his door instead of the other way around. Still, he could use some sleep. He'd be more alert if he got a few good hours. And she should be safe enough while he dozed, now that she was awake. "Be right back."

"Ok," she said, and he thought he saw something in her face that hadn't been there yesterday. Trust. She was finally starting to trust him.

The thought made his steps lighter as he headed toward the stairs.

And he was still smiling when he returned a scant twenty minutes later. But the smile quickly left his face when he saw that she'd left the door open for him. What had she been thinking?

He was halfway down the hall to her room when True growled and lunged for the door. Gabe released his grip on the leash, and he and the dog both barreled toward Kami's open suite door.

Gabe's heart pounded hard as he ran. It seemed like an eternity before he reached her suite door, although the hallway wasn't long.

"Kami?" he burst into her room, looking

around for her. The first room to the suite was empty. Nothing seemed disturbed.

True growled and headed for a closed door near the back of the suite. Since the suite mirrored the layout of his own, Gabe knew it was the bathroom.

"Gabe?" Kami shouted from inside the bathroom. "Gabe, is that you?"

Her voice broke on the last word, and she flung open the door.

"He must have been waiting for you to leave. I don't know how he found us, Gabe, but he was here. He was in the room. I locked myself in the bathroom."

She choked back a sob as tears ran down her face. "But I left your cell phone out here. I couldn't call for help, Gabe. And he was out here!"

"Slow down, Kami, take it easy. He's gone now." Gabe took her in his arms and held her close, stroking her back gently to calm her. She shook like a sapling caught in a high wind.

"Are you sure he is gone? He was here, Gabe. *Here in the room with me.*"

"I came through the suite, Kami, there's no one here. True would have found them."

The dog was busy sniffing the floor now, at something lying by the bathroom door. It looked like a crumpled sheet of paper.

"Yes," she nodded against his chest and shuddered. "Yes, you're right. True would have found him. Did you see anyone on the stairs?"

"No, I didn't see anyone. And that's the only stairway that he would have access to. He must have found a way to sneak by the staff."

She groaned against his chest.

"I was only gone twenty minutes, Kami. He can't have been here long. Are you sure it was him?"

She pushed away from him and craned her neck to look into his face, "What do you mean, am I sure it was him? Yes, I'm sure it was him. I was out here getting my toothbrush out of my bag, and I heard the door unlock. I thought it was the maid. But it wasn't. The door wasn't even open all the way, and I heard his voice. He asked if anyone was home and then said 'ready or not, here I come'. His voice was the same one on the phone."

"And?" Gabe felt tension mounting in his chest. The man had been so close to her. So close. And he'd been clever enough to wait for Gabe to go out with True. He must have stolen a key from one of the staff.

The stalker was more clever than he'd thought.

"I ran to the bathroom and locked the door. He came into the room. He asked if I was ready for him. For the things he wanted to do with me."

Her face flamed red. "Oh, he said horrible things, Gabe. Horrible, disgusting things."

Her voice broke on a sob and she turned away from him, putting her hands over her face.

"Kami, it's going to be ok." He put his hand on her shaking shoulder for comfort, but the gesture seemed too insignificant to calm the anguish she must be feeling.

"How? He's too smart, Gabe. Too smart. How did he know we were here? How did he get up here without being seen? How did he know you were gone?"

"Kami, I promise that you are going to be ok. I'm doing all I can to find him. And so is Jamie. And

Jamie is one determined woman."

She turned to look at him, wiping her eyes with the shirtsleeve of her pajamas. "Do you really think so, or are you just saying that to comfort me?"

"I really mean it, Kami. We'll just have to step up our game."

"He told me to stay away from you, Gabe, or it was going to be worse for me."

Gabe tamped down the anger simmering in his gut. "His threats are meaningless, Kami. They're only meant to scare you."

"He told me you weren't the man you were pretending to be. He said I couldn't trust you. He said you let people down." Her eyes sought his and she searched his face, almost as if looking for an assurance of his honesty.

"And do you believe him?" Gabe asked, feeling a hard cold ball of anger forming tightly in the pit of his stomach. The man had no right to do this to her. No right to terrorize her like this.

"No," she said after a very slight pause. "No, I don't believe him. I want to trust you, Gabe. Actually," she gave a small self-derisive laugh, "I need to trust you at this point. You're my lifeline right now, so I really have no choice. And you have proven to be trustworthy so far."

"Did he say anything else, Kami? Anything that would give you a clue as to why he's doing this?"

She looked uncomfortable. "He said that once he had me, he was going to marry me. And then he'd have the money and me."

"It's about the money then?"

"It's always about the money!" Anger had crept into her voice, replacing some of the fear that had been there moments ago. He was glad of the change.

"Is it? Or is it more? We need to figure out how he became fixated on you in the first place."

"How? How are we going to do that Gabe? He always seems to be one step ahead of us."

"Jamie got a full face-shot of him from your security cameras when he trashed your kitchen. Maybe she'll get a hit from one of the police databases with that. For now, we need to find out how he found you and why he was here."

She nodded at him, looking lost.

"He didn't break anything, and he didn't try to get into the bathroom with you?"

"No."

"So, he must not have come to take you, but just to scare you or get a closer look at you."

She walked over and picked up the paper True was still sniffing.

"Maybe he came to leave this?"

She opened the crumpled paper and smoothed the edges. Then read aloud from the page.

"You didn't protect Jen. You let her down and she died. You won't have any better luck keeping Kami from me."

She looked at him, a stricken expression on her face. "Who is Jen, Gabe? And what happened to her?"

Gabe knew he wasn't going to get out of explaining and still be able to keep the trust that she'd started to feel for him. He didn't even know if he'd be able to keep her trust when he told her the story. The note was right, after all, he hadn't been able to save Jen.

"Jen was my sister, Kami. She was killed by a stalker ten years ago."

"Oh, Gabe, that's awful! I'm so sorry!"

"I was with the police force at the time. I tried to protect her. But he got to her just the same. I thought I had every angle covered, but he found a way to get to her. And she put up one heck of a fight, but he killed her anyway. It was a senseless brutal murder."

Kami's face blanched of all color, and he could see that his story of failure had frightened her even more, but she still came closer and tentatively took his hand as if to offer comfort.

"I'm ashamed to admit I went a little crazy after that, Kami. I started drinking, I got kicked off of the force for bad behavior, and I did a lot of things I'm not proud of. The one thing I did do was to find her stalker. He's behind bars now, so I know it isn't the same man who is terrorizing you."

"And that's when you became a private investigator?" She asked as she patted the back of his hand as one might do to a bereft child.

He couldn't help but think that she was taking this all too well.

"Yes, it is. I couldn't go back to the force, but I still wanted to help people."

"And so the reason he said you couldn't be trusted is because you weren't able to stop your sister's murder?"

He swallowed hard and then admitted to his greatest failing, "Yes."

She stepped a bit closer and enveloped him in a tentative hug. "Oh, Gabe, that's so unfair. It wasn't your fault!"

"If only I believed that, Kami. But I know that it was. If only I'd been more vigilant, she would be alive today." He felt the weight of his own words

69

pressing down on his shoulders, the heavy weight of failure and loss and helplessness.

"Gabe," she looked up at him, her arms still around him. "It wasn't your fault. You were not the one who committed such a heinous act. He was, and he's responsible. "

"But, Kami, she was my sister. I should have tried harder. I should have done something more. I shouldn't have let her die."

"I'm sure you did all that you could, Gabe. Just like you are doing for me. You need to forgive yourself. God forgives all sins, and so surely you can forgive yourself and leave this guilt behind?"

She gave him one last squeeze and stepped back, sniffing. Her eyes were still bright with tears, but he couldn't tell if it was from her earlier scare or from compassion.

Chapter Twelve

"Here it is," Gabe mumbled as he crawled out from under her old Mercury holding something small and black between his fingers. "It is a GPS tracker."

"It's so small! How did you know it was there?" She took the tiny device from him as he climbed to his feet. It was round, barely the circumference of a quarter, and only about an inch high, with a bright blinking red light on the top.

He paused to bend over and dust off his pants. "It was the only logical explanation. He had to have planted a tracker on you or one of your possessions. I thought I'd search the car first, since it was the most obvious place."

"Now what?" she asked.

He took the device from her fingers, smiling as he dropped it onto the pavement and crushed it beneath his heel. "Now, we find another place to stay."

She nodded. "I've already checked us out. And I put my bag in the back seat. And yours too."

"Thanks, I'll have Jamie come pick up my car today. We can just take yours. And, if you want to call anyone, now's the time since he already knows our location. Use your regular phone, though, not the new one."

She nodded and pulled her phone from her pocket.

"It wouldn't hurt to call the police and give them an update. But I'll do it if you'd rather not."

"No, no, I'll do it," she promised, feeling a bit overwhelmed at the way he was taking charge. But, she had to admit, she had no idea what she would have done without him.

"So, what city do you feel like visiting? We're going to get out of town for a while." He grinned at her.

"We are?" She asked.

"Just think of it as a mini vacation."

It had been a good long while since she'd had a vacation. Not that she had a lot to escape from since she'd inherited her grandfather's money. And she'd had no one to go on vacation with since her parents had died. The last time she'd gone on anything resembling a vacation was when she was a kid and they'd all gone on a camping trip.

She had such fond memories of that time.

"Okay. So we're going to take off, just like that?"

"Sure, I'll call in some favors and get everything taken care of while we're gone. I'm sure Stan wouldn't mind keeping an eye on our houses. And he'd probably know some folks who would help clean the mess in your kitchen. Jamie will keep tabs on my agency while I'm out and I can keep on top of things from any location, as long as I have cell service. I'll just need to stop by and pick up my laptop so Jamie can use it to show me what magic she's been working in our absence. And you'll need to stop by the bank and get some cash. We don't want a paper trail."

She nodded, feeling overwhelmed again.

Please, Lord, help me get through this, she prayed silently.

She took a deep breath, feeling comforted that she could pray to the One who was all powerful, and thought about her predicament for a moment, then decided that it was all a matter of perspective. She could choose to feel frightened and terrorized, chased from her home by an insane man and crowded out of her own city by his actions. Or, she could trust in the Lord and try to look for the hidden blessing in all of this.

She just might enjoy a vacation. Gabe wasn't such a bad companion, and while they were travelling, they would have a better chance of throwing the stalker off guard and staying one step ahead of him.

Perhaps the stalker would even decide that she wasn't worth the trouble and forget about her?

"How does Hawaii sound? I've always wanted to see it!! We could take a cruise!"

"Hawaii? Cruise? Um…" Gabe suddenly looked uncomfortable. "I was thinking more along the lines of a long drive and an extended stay in an affordable, out of the way cabin. "

She felt the grin fade from her face. He *had* asked her where she wanted to go. She felt a little awkward at her enthusiasm now. "Well, I guess that would be ok too."

"Great. That's much easier on the budget!" Gabe looked very relieved.

She couldn't help but laugh at him now. It wasn't the location that he objected to, it was the expense.

"Gabe, if it's alright, I'd rather go to Hawaii. If it is all about the expense, then please, don't worry. I'll pay for everything."

He looked a little squeamish. "I can't ask you to do that, Kami. It wouldn't be right."

"But you didn't ask, I offered. Please, let me do this, you've done so much for me already."

He looked like he was trying to swallow a lemon, rind and all. His mouth puckered with indecision. He frowned.

"I don't think…" he began.

She didn't want to give him the chance to object. Now that she'd thought about it a little, she really wanted that vacation. Even if it was with a semi-stranger like Gabe.

"Please, Gabe, I really want to see Hawaii. And it will get us away, far away, from the stalker. Don't you agree?"

He paused a moment before shaking his head, "I suppose. Hawaii is a long way for a stalker to go. And, with the expense involved in a last minute Hawaiian cruise, I doubt he'll be able to follow us. Are you sure you don't mind the expense?"

She laughed, "Gabe, the money my grandfather left me has been more of a burden than a relief. I wouldn't mind spending some of it in this way. Besides, he had so many investments that I could live for the rest of my life without working and never worry about running out of money. My grandfather was a very shrewd man."

Gabe hated to waste money, and he said the first thing that came to his mind. "But what about your children? Don't you plan to have children, Kami? Don't you want to leave anything to them?"

"Children?" It was her turn to frown. "Well,

since Logan and I..." she paused, not wanting to tell him about Logan. "Let's just say that I haven't really thought about children for a while. I've realized that children just weren't a blessing that I would probably ever have."

His gaze softened. "Someday, I want a house full of children."

"You do?" she asked, surprised. What man wanted a houseful of children? In her experience, men were too selfish to want children. They basically seemed to want the world to be their playground, not giving a thought to sharing that playground with their children. Of course, there were exceptions, like Stan, but they were few and far between. And Kami had given up finding one of them to share her life with.

He laughed. "You seem surprised. Of course I do. I want to leave a legacy. I want to know that when I'm gone, I'll have done some good in this world by having some children and teaching them Christ's ways. So that they, in turn, can teach their children, and their children's children. The way it is supposed to be."

Kami's heart gave a sudden lurch. That's exactly how she used to feel about it – before she had realized that it probably wasn't going to happen for her. She'd wanted the white picket fence, the loving husband, and the rosy-cheeked children. But her dreams for that had gone up in smoke after Logan. And she had written them off as unrealistic. To hear Gabe speak aloud her heart's desire made her want to weep and hug him at the same time.

She was becoming less and less certain that she'd get out of this situation with her heart intact. By the time the stalker was caught, she might be head over heels in love with Gabe. She fought her reckless heart, though. Choosing to focus on the moment at hand.

"I've always felt that way, too. I just didn't know that anyone else had." She said the words softly, almost afraid to speak them aloud and share her dream with him.

He gave her a look that she couldn't quite interpret. Surprise, yes, but mixed with another emotion that she thought might be something other than the simple Christian kindness that he'd shown her so far.

"Hawaii it is, then?" he asked.

She was grateful for the change of subject.

"Yes, let's do that. But what about True? Even if they'd let him on the cruise ship – which I doubt – I don't think he'd enjoy it very much."

Gabe winked at her, "I know the perfect place for him. Trust me. Stan's kids will *love* having him over!"

She laughed at his expression of mock wickedness, "But what about Stan?"

He laughed too. "Stan, perhaps not so much. But I hear his wife is a big fan of Shepherds. Been after him for years to get the kids a dog. Now maybe True will show him just how much fun it is to have one around. And, with True, he gets an added bonus. Not many dogs are as highly trained as True."

He reached down and rubbed the dog behind the ears as if in encouragement.

"Don't worry, boy," she crooned bending down to pat True's heavy side. "You'll enjoy the children."

True whined as if in agreement, then turned to the side so she could scratch his favorite spot on his rear end.

Kami laughed aloud, realizing that despite the dire situation, True and Gabe had managed to make her feel more alive than she had in a good long while.

***

Kami was amazed at just how easy their plans fell into place. Stan was more than happy to dog-sit for them, and agreed happily to housesit as well. He had made a few calls and found a veritable army to help clean up the destruction in her kitchen, and Kami left him with a large amount of cash to pay each volunteer and to pay for any repairs that were needed. He'd protested the extreme amount, but she'd explained the stipulation in her grandfather's will that prohibited charity. After a little talking, she'd been able to get him to agree to the outrageous payment for services as a way to get around the problem, while still helping out the people in the church at the same time. It wasn't charity if they were being paid for work they performed.

She'd had no trouble making the travel arrangements – and discovered once again that money could open almost any door. Except, she mused, the one to happiness. It seemed that since she'd first inherited her grandfather's money, that door had remained firmly closed.

When the surprised travel agent had learned that money was no object, the plans for the trip had been quickly finalized. They were booked in first class cabins on the Regent Seven Seas line and now had first class airfare to their embarking destination in Seattle.

Kami silently thanked God for the blessing of her grandfather's money when she hung up the phone with the travel agent. Without it, escape from the stalker would have been much more difficult. It was the first time that she could remember that she thought of the money more of a blessing than a burden.

"Finally off the phone? That didn't take as long as I thought. Just one more quick stop by my office to grab my laptop, and then we are off." Gabe's voice cut into her musings.

"Will I get to meet Jamie at your office? I'd like to thank her for all she'd done for me so far."

"I hope so. I called her to let her know we'd be stopping by, but Jamie keeps her own hours, so you just never know. I'm fairly certain she'll be there since she said she had something to share with me."

Kami nodded. "It was harder than I thought to leave True with Stan. It is amazing how fast we can become attached, isn't it?"

Gabe gave her another unreadable look as he glanced sideways at her. "Yes, yes it is amazing how fast that happens. But, don't worry about True. Stan's wife will take good care of him. Did you see how delighted she was when we brought him in the house?"

Kami chuckled at the memory of the expression on the woman's face, and Stan's too. "Yes, I do. I don't think I'll forget Stan's expression any time soon, either. He seemed a little daunted by True's size."

"Yes, but once you showed him True's training, he seemed eager enough to have him around." Gabe turned the Mercury into a small parking lot in front of a rather run-down building.

"I think it was the kids' reaction that did that."

To Kami's surprise, Gabe pulled the Mercury into a spot in front of the building, put it in park, killed the engine and announced, "Well, here we are.

The Mathews Agency."

Kami tried to hide her reaction from him. His agency was in a bit of disrepair. It needed a good coat of paint and a new sidewalk. The one in front of his office was cracked and broken in several areas. The building practically screamed "low rent" which wasn't at all the mental image that she'd had of his agency. She could see that there had been a few careful repairs done, but not enough to lift the building completely out of its state of disrepair.

Gabe seemed to know what she was thinking, "It isn't much, but it is what I could afford. Some day I'll finish all of the repairs, but I don't have anyone lining up at my door right now, so that day may have to wait a while longer."

His tone was just the slightest bit defensive.

Chagrined, she looked away from his intense gaze. Here she was throwing money at all of her problems without thought as to what *his* financial situation was. She'd never given it a second thought. But now, she could see that Gabe wasn't exactly flush in the pockets. For what she'd spent in the last few days on True, the hotel and the travel arrangements, she could, no doubt, have purchased a whole new building for his agency.

Not a bad idea!

She hid a grin at the thought. It wouldn't be charity if she was compensating him for helping her out with her stalker problem, now would it? When – if – everything was back to normal, she silently vowed to get him a better place, or at least make sure he had enough to fix up the one he had. He should have an agency he didn't have to feel defensive about. One that would attract cases to his door so that he could help more people as he'd helped her. He was good at what he did, and he should be able to share that skill with people without the burden of financial worry hanging over his shoulder.

Remembering their earlier conversation, she felt a twinge at her conscience. She'd accused him of helping only for the money, and he'd said that there would be *no money involved.* She'd just have to decide differently. He didn't have to know it until the job was done. Offering him money now that she's seen his agency would only wound his pride. No wonder he'd balked at the trip to Hawaii and the expense involved. Clearly, there was no way he could currently afford it.

"No one lining up? They just don't know what they're missing!" She grinned at him to lighten the mood.

He gave her a grin back, and for the second time since she'd met him, Kami noticed how nice his smile was. His expression, since she'd met him, had usually been very serious, as if his mind was constantly occupied with things of vital importance. Which, she had to admit, in his line of work it probably was. But when he smiled, his face lit up and he seemed more carefree.

"Jamie's car is here, so you'll get your wish. Prepare to be amazed. Jamie is like no one you've ever met before."

Kami wondered exactly what he meant by that as she followed him inside.

"Hey'a boss!" A very thin woman greeted Gabe as he walked through the door. She was seated behind an enormous desk, which was stacked high with chaotic piles of manila folders and mail, all piled haphazardly around six flat-screen computer monitors.

Dressed casually in jeans, sneakers and a designer sweater, with her hair pulled back in a messy ponytail and dark rimmed reading glasses perched on her nose, she managed to pull off the look of being chic, with a side of nerdy.

"Hey, Jamie, glad you're here," Gabe greeted the woman warmly.

"And you must be Kami?" Jamie asked as she stood up, tossed her reading glasses onto a pile of folders and moving out from behind the desk. "I'm glad to meet you and see you safe and sound in person. You've had a rough couple of days of it, haven't you?"

Kami nodded, surprised at the compassion she saw in the other woman's eyes.

"Well, Gabe here will take good care of you. He's the best," Jamie gave Gabe a playful punch in the shoulder. "Although he doesn't seem to know it yet. Which is a good thing. Keeps him humble. I couldn't work for a guy who was stuck on himself, y'know?"

"Actually, since we're playing admiration society here, we might as well be honest," Gabe said. "Jamie is a genius with computers, and she's sort of the glue that keeps this agency running. So, she just makes me look good."

He grinned as Jamie blushed.

"You're too kind. A genius, huh?" Her wide grin said that she was pleased with his compliments, though.

Kami could see that their friendship was genuine and deep. It made her long for a friend of her own.

"Speaking of computers, boy do I have some good stuff for you! Wait till you see this!" She motioned them around so that they could look at the bank of monitors from behind her desk while she took a seat.

"I missed it the first few times I watched the tapes. The guy who was on the security tapes wasn't alone!" She grabbed the mouse, brought up the security footage and in a few clicks they were watching a video of Kami's house.

The footage rolled on for several minutes, showing a clear view of her front lawn and the evergreens that bordered her yard on the south side, before a dark blob appeared out of nowhere and the camera footage suddenly cut off.

"See? Did you see that?" Jamie stopped the video and turned to look at them expectantly.

"I didn't see anything but a dark blob," Kami said, wondering why Jamie found that to be such good news.

"Rewind it a bit?" Gabe asked.

Jamie happily complied, seeming really excited about her find.

"Yes, I see them. They're hard to pick out. See, look, Kami. There in the trees. There's not one, but two men, hiding. In separate trees. It doesn't look like they even realize the other is there."

"I missed them the first few times through the footage, because I was concentrating on the guy who took out the security cameras and trashed the kitchen."

"Three men? I have *three* stalkers?" Kami asked, feeling the blood rush to her head at the realization. One stalker was hard enough to deal with, but three? Who had three stalkers anyway?

"Not three stalkers, Kami. I think that's highly unlikely. Stalkers work alone. And while

82

these guys here in the trees," Gabe pointed to the monitor, "don't seem to know that the other one is present, they certainly get an eye-full of the other guy when he breaks the camera. We know they saw him do that. This changes things," Gabe said.

"Yeah, I'll say," Jamie chimed in. "It changes things in a big way."

"How?" Kami was about to burst from not knowing. Was this a good or a bad thing? It had to be bad to have three men trying to get to her.

"The footage of the two men gives us a clear reason to believe that you don't have any stalkers at all, Kami, which is a good thing. But, the question is, *why* would you have two men lurking in the trees around your house while a third breaks in? And none of them seem to be working together," Jamie explained.

"Well, we can't rule out that one of the men in the trees may be working with the one who broke the camera. That's a possibility. He could have been the lookout." Gabe pointed out.

"True," Jamie nodded and stared at the monitors on her desk thoughtfully. "But we still need to find out why there would be three men there. Kami, can you think of anyone who would have a motive to hire someone to harass you?"

"Of course, both my aunt and my uncle have a grudge against me. Because of the way my grandfather wrote his will. I had nothing to do with his decision, but they both hate me. It is compounded by the fact that my grandfather also wrote in the will that I was not allowed to give them the money to make things better."

Jamie nodded, "I guess that could be it. A few million dollars and change would be a good reason to hire someone to hurt you."

"Kami, who gets the money if you should die?" Gabe suddenly asked, looking concerned.

"That part wasn't mentioned in Grandfather's will. And I don't have a will of my own, so I guess no one gets it."

Jamie and Gabe shared a look.

"That's not necessarily true, Kami. Your closest surviving relatives would be in line to get the money. In court, your aunt and uncle would probably get it, even thought your grandfather's will specifies that you cannot *give* them the money. It says nothing about them inheriting it if you should die." Gabe told her.

Kami felt lightheaded at the realization of what that meant. "Oh my! That means…"

Gabe and Jamie both looked sympathetic.

Gabe put his hand on her shoulder as if in support.

Jamie finished her sentence for her, "That means that quite possibly your aunt, or uncle, or both have hired multiple people to try to kill you, Kami."

But she really didn't need to finish the thought out loud, Kami knew they must all be thinking the same thing. She was in a lot of trouble.

How many had been hired to do the job? She couldn't know. Gabe couldn't know.

"I'll never be safe again," she whispered. "Grandfather's money is such a burden!"

"It will be ok, Kami. Gabe will protect you," Jamie stood and turned around to face her. "And I have an idea."

"We're open to suggestions," Gabe announced.

Kami just stood there feeling numb. Stunned

at the thought that her aunt and uncle might hate her enough to hire someone to have her killed. Just because of the *money.*

"We can't be sure, though, right? I mean, they might *not* have hired someone to do this? Surely they can't hate me that much. They're the only family I have left. I thought that some day, perhaps, they might be open to reconciliation."

Gabe's eyes held compassion when he looked at her, it was almost more than she could bear at the moment. The thought that a man like Gabe, a virtual stranger, and his employee might care for her more than her own family almost brought tears to her eyes. The money her grandfather had left her was like a poison seeping into her relationships. She was glad that it hadn't tainted Gabe and Jamie.

"We can't be sure, no. But, Jamie is right, a few million dollars can cause a lot of hate."

"Kami, don't loose hope, I have a plan. And it is really quite simple. Gabe can protect you while we work on finding the identities of the three men in this video, and while he's doing that, you can make your own will. If you name a beneficiary, and let it be known to your aunt and uncle that the beneficiary is *not* them, then they'll have no reason to think that they'll get the money if you're out of the picture."

"True," Gabe nodded. "It's a good plan, Kami. If they know that they don't have a chance to get the money, then they'll have no reason to send anyone after you."

"Yes, but we still don't know for sure that it's them," Kami was still unwilling to believe that her aunt and uncle would go to such lengths to get the money. They were angry, but they weren't killers. Were they?

"That's right. We can look into that. But right now, it is the best answer we have to explain what's going on. And, having a will isn't a bad idea, Kami. It can't hurt in any case."

Kami suddenly came to another realization. She had no one to leave the money to. As the only child of deceased parents, she had no family other than her aunt and uncle, and if what Jamie said was true, she couldn't leave the money to them. Her former friends had deserted her when the media had done such a good job of portraying her as a money-grubber, and she hadn't dared to try to make any new ones. She couldn't give it to charity, either. So who? She didn't have any close friends. She couldn't leave it to the church. There was no one who cared about her.

Except Gabe. And Jamie. And Stan.

She looked at them, standing there, knowing that Gabe was willing to put his life on the line to help her, and Jamie was as well. It was a good enough reason for her.

"I have another problem," Kami told them. "I have no one to leave the money to. Except perhaps, you."

Both Gabe and Jamie stared at her.

Gabe looked stunned.

Jamie's face went through a series of emotions, from surprise to anxiety before finally settling on sympathy.

"Aw, Kami. No one? No friends or family other than your aunt and uncle?"

Kami shook her head, surprised at Jamie's reaction. Surprised that instead of focusing on the money, she had instead focused on the fact that Kami was essentially alone in the world.

"I'm sorry, Hon. That really stinks," Jamie stepped forward and awkwardly enfolded her in an embrace.

Kami returned the embrace tentatively. She wasn't used to displays of affection from complete strangers, but Jamie's embrace seemed to be a genuine show of understanding.

"I don't want your money, though, Kami," Jamie said. "Give it to Gabe. From what I can see, that money has been nothing but trouble for you, but I think Gabe can handle any trouble or temptation it sends his way. Not so sure about myself."

Giving her one last squeeze, Jamie stepped back. "But, Hon, I can be here for you if you need a friend. You could use one about now if I'm not wrong?"

Kami nodded, her throat getting tight with emotion. An offer of friendship from a person who had just turned down a share of millions of dollars? It was more than she'd ever have hoped for. Someone willing to be her friend despite the money.

"I don't know what to say," her voice cracked embarrassingly.

"Hey, no sweat, you don't have to say anything. Just call if you need a little girl-talk, okay? Gabe can give you my number. And, while you're in Hawaii, eat some poi for me. I've always wondered how it tastes." Jamie grinned as if trying to diffuse the emotional tension hanging in the air.

"Kami," Gabe's voice held a wealth of emotion. "I-"

She cut him off, "Please, Gabe, don't argue. I don't have anyone else. And besides, Jamie's right, you can handle any problems that it brings."

Gabe rubbed the back of his neck with one

hand, his lips compressed into a tight line. She could tell that he didn't think it was right, and he was trying not to say anything that would hurt her feelings.

"Well, you can do what you think is right, but I don't want your money either. Jamie's right, though, you *do* need to make a will and the beneficiary shouldn't be your aunt and uncle. Tell you what, if you do put me in the will and something *does* happen," he winced slightly as he said it, as if he just couldn't stand the thought of anything happening to her. "I'll give the money to the church for you, okay?"

"Okay," she agreed.

"Okay," Jamie clapped her hands and rubbed them together as if the simple gesture could clear the air of the emotional tensions it has suddenly gathered. "Now that that's taken care of, we need to get the plan in motion. When do you leave for Hawaii?"

"In seven days," Kami answered.

When Gabe looked at her in surprise, she gave him a half-hearted smile. "I'm sorry, I know you wanted to leave right away, and I was going to tell you. The ship doesn't leave until then, and I thought we'd just stay in a few random hotels in Seattle until boarding. Is that going to be alright?"

"Sure," Gabe nodded, but a frown still shadowed his face. "I was just planning on leaving sooner. I should have asked."

"Well," Jamie gave Gabe a look. "If you leave today and stay in a few random hotels in Seattle, that should be virtually the same thing as getting on the ship. He, I mean *they*, will still have a hard time finding you."

Gabe nodded and then promptly changed the subject, and Kami couldn't tell if he was angry about the delay or the fact that she hadn't told him yet, or if he was merely concerned about protecting her until they got on the ship. "Did Stan's buddy come up with anything on the guy in Kami's kitchen?"

"No," Jamie shook her head. "Not yet."

The front door of the agency swung open and a man entered.

"Is this the Mathews Agency?" he asked.

"Sure is," Jamie answered. "Can we help you with something?"

"Yes. I'm not interrupting anything, am I?" He gestured to the three of them standing there.

Kami thought he seemed a little nervous and wondered vaguely why he'd come to Gabe for help. What sorts of people did Gabe help anyway? Was this man someone trying to find out if his spouse was cheating on him, or was his problem more serious? Perhaps a runaway child?

"No, no. You're fine," Jamie stepped around the side of the desk and approached the man. "Come on in and have a seat. We're almost finished."

Instead of following her directive, the man looked pointedly at Gabe.

"Are you Gabe Mathews, then?" he asked.

Kami thought she saw a flicker of something – anger? Resentment? Fear? – in the man's gaze as he looked at Gabe, but she couldn't be sure what it was.

"Yes," Gabe answered, stepping around Kami to approach the man.

The man smiled, then he pulled a Taser from his pocket and shot the electrodes right into Gabe's chest.

Kami squelched a scream as Gabe hit the floor, his heavy body twitching uncontrollably at her feet.

Jamie took two running steps and attempted to knock the Taser out of the man's hand. She succeeded, but he shoved her backward before she could do anything else.

She tumbled into the row of wooden chairs just under the front plate-glass windows, a grunt of pain escaping her mouth as she landed awkwardly on top of the chairs.

Kami felt as if her feet were frozen to the floor for a second. Horror gripped her.

He's here for me!

She looked frantically around for anything to use as a weapon. Nothing!

She picked up the only thing within reach – Jamie's wireless keyboard – and turned to the man, brandishing the keyboard like a baseball bat.

He laughed and stepping around Gabe's body toward her.

She threw the keyboard at his head and darted sideways, putting Jamie's desk between them.

Jamie groaned and climbed to her feet, staggering toward the desk, "Run, Kami!"

Adrenalin pumped through her and she was tempted to bolt as Jamie instructed, but she didn't want to leave Gabe and Jamie at the mercy of the man. What if he had a gun? What if he shot them?

He pulled another Taser from his pocket. She shrieked and hunched down behind Jamie's computer monitors, skittering to the side as she did so.

"Not gonna help," the man said.

Jamie was at her side in an instant, jerking on her arm. "We've got to go!"

"But," Kami glanced at Gabe's feet sticking out from the other side of the desk.

"Now!" Jamie hissed, pulling her toward the

door just as the man sent the monitors flying off the desk with a sweep of his arm.

Kami turned to run with Jamie.

A burning sensation nailed her in the back, just between her shoulder blades, then the awful feeling of five thousand volts slamming into her nervous system overtook any thought of fleeing that she might have had. Blackness swam at the edges of her vision as her head slammed into the floor.

She thought she heard the man laugh as she lost consciousness.

Chapter Thirteen

"We've got to find her!" Gabe paced back and forth in his office area, angry with himself for letting Kami slip through his fingers.

"There was nothing we could have done, Gabe," Jamie rubbed her sore neck muscles with her spare hand, right above the area that the assailant had shot her with the Taser he'd been carrying.

Gabe could commiserate; he had a sore spot on his chest that must feel the same way. The man had come prepared, that's all he could say. Too bad they hadn't been quite as ready for him.

"Try to calm down, Gabe, I've never seen you like this," Jamie said.

"Calm down? My client has just been taken *from my office* by an unknown assailant. Her life is probably in danger. How can I calm down?"

Jamie gave him a look, "You know what I mean. You can't think clearly when you're like this, and we need you thinking clearly! I'm as upset as you are that Kami was taken right out from under our noses."

"Did you get a look at his vehicle?" Gabe asked, hoping for a shred of evidence to point them in the right direction.

"I'm sorry, no, I didn't. I was out cold just like you."

"Cell phone GPS signal?"

"Already checked. Her phone must be turned off, or he disposed of it somehow. No signal. *But* I *did* install a webcam near the entrance a couple of weeks ago."

Gabe whirled around to stare at her, "You did? Then what are we doing standing here? We could be looking through the footage!"

"Gabe, the guy trashed my monitors when he trashed my desk! I'm downloading a backup from the server to your laptop as we speak, but it will take a few moments. You should take this time to say a prayer and get your head in the right place. You know how to let go and let God, so do it. We'll do the best we can, but you'll have to trust Him to protect her until we can find her, okay?"

Gabe nodded. It was true. He wasn't relying on his faith, and in the face of such a lack of evidence to go on, it was all he had. He sat down heavily in his chair, closed his eyes and said a quick, silent prayer.

Please help me, Lord, to help her. Protect her and keep her safe until she can be found.

After a moment, he was able to collect his rushing thoughts.

"You know, if the man had wanted her dead, then surely he would have taken care of that when he was here instead of using a Taser on her. If he was a killer, why would he do that?"

"Good point," Jamie nodded at him. "And, for that matter, why did he spare us? He could have shot the both of us with something other than a Taser, but he didn't."

She came around the side of his desk, shoving

his laptop in front of him.

"Here's the backup of the webcam feed. The guy was driving a green Ford Expedition, and the webcam got a good shot of his plate. It also got a good shot of his face when he entered, and it shows him putting Kami in his SUV and heading west."

Gabe jumped up out of his chair, "Jamie, I know I've said it before, but this time it might just literally be true, you're a life saver!"

"Go get the girl, Gabe. I'll call in the incident to the police, give them the plate number and send over a still shot of his face. Hopefully, they'll be able to give you some help."

"Thanks," Gabe muttered as he rushed out the door on legs still weak and twitchy from electric shock. Just knowing that they were going "west" wasn't much to go on, but the guy didn't have that much of a lead. Maybe twenty minutes. With a little help, he might just be able to find them before anything more happened.

The speed limit didn't seem fast enough as he peeled out of his agency parking lot, but he tried his best to stay under it as he headed west. Traffic was light until he hit Ridge Road, then it tightened up a bit. He searched through the traffic for the green Expedition.

His phone rang and he quickly answered it, thinking it must be Jamie. "Hello?"

"Gabe?"

The voice was barely more than a whisper, but Gabe recognized it as Kami's.

"Kami? Thank God! Are you all right? Where are you?"

"He didn't take my phone away and he doesn't know I've turned it on. He thinks I'm still unconscious. He tossed me in the back of his SUV. I have to be quiet."

"Where are you, Kami? Can you tell where you are?" Gabe tried to modulate his voice, to keep his fear for her from coming through the phone. She didn't need to know how worried he was about her.

"I can only catch a glimpse now and then through the window, but I think we're in the Old Town area. We passed the Museum of World Treasures just a few minutes ago. I saw the top of the building from the SUV."

"Are you ok, Kami?" If the man had hurt her, he would never forgive himself.

"I'm ok, Gabe, except for a headache. Please, just help me!"

"I'm trying, Kami. I'm trying. I need you to hang up with me and call 911. They can use the GPS on your phone to track you. Tell them just what you told me, that you have to be quiet. Then try to hide your phone if he stops."

"Okay," she whispered, her breath catching.

Gabe winced, knowing she had stifled a sob.

"Don't cry, Kami. The Lord is with you. You'll be ok," he assured her, right before she hung up.

He said another quick prayer and took the next left, heading towards Old Town.

He called Jamie, pressing speed dial, and when she answered, he didn't give her much time to talk, "Jamie, Kami called me, she's ok so far. He hasn't hurt her yet. They're still driving. Yes, yes. Can you get her GPS coordinates for me since she's turned on her phone? I've told her to call 911 and have them do the same."

"Yes, I can do that! Just a minute." He heard

Jamie typing frantically. "Boss, when this is over, you gotta get a new laptop. This one is so slow!"

He should have replaced that laptop months ago, but he just hadn't had the funds. He'd used what he had in the budget for Jamie's computers. He'd thought at the time that it was a much better investment, since she got so much more out of her computers than he did. Now he wished he'd have sprung for a new one just for the few extra seconds it might have given them.

"Got it!" Jamie screeched in his ear a moment later, her voice high with excitement. "Her signal is heading north now. It shows he's on I-135. And the police scanner said that there are several patrol cars heading that way now, so he'll be having company any moment."

Gabe's heart pounded. If the man ran from the police it could be bad. If there was a high-speed chase on the highway, they could all end up in an accident. Kami could be killed.

"We need to pray," Gabe choked out into the phone.

He was coming to realize that there were things he should have said to Kami earlier. He should have told her he was coming to care for her. Now, faced with the fact that he might never see her again, he realized that not sharing his feeling had been a mistake. He wanted her in his life for a good long while. Not just because of the case. But because of who she was. And now he might not get the chance to tell her that.

Lord, please guide my actions and those of the police and help us to help Kami. Please keep her safe!

He heard Jamie murmuring a prayer in his ear

and he was grateful. *Where two or more are gathered in my name...* Mathew 18:20 had never before offered such comfort to him.

As he approached the on-ramp for I-135, he could hear sirens screaming down the Interstate ahead of him. He realized that he wasn't too far behind them.

"Where are they now?" he asked Jamie.

"I've started tracking your GPS as well. You're not more than two miles away from her signal, Gabe. The police are closing in. On the scanner, one of them just called for more backup. The guy's going to try to run, Gabe."

Gabe heard his own horror reflected in Jamie's voice.

A high-speed chase on the Interstate was just bad news all around. It would be difficult to catch the guy without causing an accident.

His heart hammering in his throat, and adrenaline surged through him as he wove through the slower traffic trying to catch up to Kami.

He knew he didn't have a chance though. The police and the SUV were all going faster than he was. His sedan just wasn't made for high-speed chases.

Still, he planned to try to be close when the chase ended. Kami would need him to be there for her.

Plowing through traffic, Gabe kept the phone to his ear, listening to Jamie's blow-by-blow updates as they were reported on the scanner.

"They're close now, Gabe. They've got him boxed in. Only a mile ahead of your location!"

Gabe pressed the accelerator harder, inching the speedometer up to a dangerous level.

"Slow down!" Jamie screeched in his ear

again. "You can't be caught speeding, and your GPS signal is going way to fast for you to be legal right now!"

"Right," Gabe growled into the phone, knowing she was correct. It was agonizing to be on the tail end of the chase.

Suddenly, he realized that it was all going to happen without him whether he wanted it that way or not. There was nothing he could do to change the outcome of the chase. Nothing. He couldn't save Kami. He couldn't comfort her in this moment of what was sure to be pure terror for her. He could only pray, and put his faith and trust in the Lord.

He felt the bunched muscles in his neck and shoulders relax as he realized this fact. The tension that he'd been holding inside slowly eased as he mentally turned over his burdens to God. His fear for Kami remained, but it was tempered by the knowledge that the Lord would make all things work for the good of those who loved Him. And Gabe was comforted by the fact that he knew that Kami loved the Lord.

A couple more police cars were coming up at his rear, but Gabe managed to keep a hold on his moment of peace and pull over like a law-abiding citizen. He resumed following them as soon as they passed, quickly building his speed back up to just under the legal speed limit.

Ahead, he could see what looked like a whole fleet of police cars, lights flashing in a miasma of blue and red.

"He's pulled over, Gabe. The scanner said that the suspect is exiting the vehicle. He's not resisting arrest!" Jamie reported, sounding overjoyed.

"Thank God!" Gabe rejoiced with her.

"They've found Kami in the back of the SUV. They're taking her out now. She's ok and they're not calling for an ambulance."

Gabe neared the scene. Police cars surrounded the green Expedition, and Gabe could see several officers leading a man in handcuffs toward a police car. Kami was surrounded by another group of officers.

He slowed his sedan, parking carefully at the side of the road to avoid traffic.

"Gabe!" Kami saw him immediately.

At her cry of recognition, an officer waved him closer.

"Gabe," Kami detached herself from the group of officers and hurried closer to him.

He could see that her face was wet with tears, but she was smiling.

When she was near enough, she surprised him by throwing her arms around him and burying her face in his chest.

"That was so terrifying, Gabe!" Her voice caught and her arms clenched tight around his middle.

"I'm so glad you are all right, Kami. It could have been much, much worse."

He hugged her back, cradling her in the circle of his arms and reveling in the feel of her safe and sound, and in his arms. He had so much he wanted to say, but he realized that it just wasn't the right time. His thoughts were a jumble in his head, all of the things that he had realized he should have said to her sooner. They built up with some urgency in his mind, because of the knowledge that, but for the grace of God, he might not have had another chance to say them to her at all. But he pushed them away, knowing that she needed some time to get over the scare she'd just had before he could talk of his feelings for her. They both did.

"One down, two to go, huh?" She pulled back slightly to look up into his face and gave him a watery smile as she joked.

She was obviously trying to inject some levity into the situation, and Gabe was proud of her for trying, and at the same time her bravery just made him want to put her away some place safe and protect her for the rest of her life so she never had to endure anything that awful again.

"Yeah, something like that," he smiled back at her, hoping that his pent up emotions would not show in his eyes. She didn't need that burden right now. "Kami, don't worry about them now. You're safe and, right now, that's all that matters."

He held her closer, and she rested her cheek against his chest again. He could feel that she still trembled with the shock of what had happened. He kissed her softly on the crown of her head, realizing that he liking the texture of her soft hair against his face.

"Thank God that you're safe," he murmured into her hair.

She sniffed, "Yes, thank God."

Chapter Fourteen

Kami felt wrung out and emotionally exhausted by the time that they arrived back at the Mathews Agency. Gabe had helped her through the ordeal at the police station when she'd given her statement, and brought her back to the agency to deal with the matter of her will. Finishing her will was only a precaution, since new developments at the police station had given her hope that her ordeal might soon be over. She hoped that she was up for completing her will, because, at the moment, all she wanted was a hot bath and a little time with a soft pillow.

Gabe reached over and took her hand before they got out of his sedan.

"We should talk before we go inside," he told her, an unfathomable look in his deep blue eyes.

She looked down that their gently entwined fingers and was grateful again for the emotional support that he'd offered her throughout the aftermath of her kidnapping. She didn't know what she would have done without his steady strength to lean on. She squeezed his calloused hand lightly and swallowed the dry lump in her throat. Before he said what he had to say, she really ought to tell him how she had begun to feel about him. On the wild ride in the SUV, she'd come to the stunning realization that she might never see him again, and that realization had rattled her. She was determined now to fully live her life, and quit hiding behind the barriers that she'd erected to keep people out and not allow them to hurt her emotionally. Part of fully living her life included telling Gabe how she felt about him. And she'd realized that her feeling for him ran deep.

"Gabe," she wasn't sure it was the right time, as exhausted and emotionally spent as she felt, but experiencing the regret that she had earlier, when she thought that she might not have another opportunity to say the things she'd left unsaid, spurred her onward. "I want to thank you for all that you've done for me. I want you to know that I'm very grateful. And, I think I should tell you that I've begun to care for you. I realized earlier that I should have told you sooner, but I was afraid that-"

"You don't need to say more," Gabe interrupted her, looking into her face earnestly. "I feel the same. I've come to care for you too, more than just as a client. You've become so important to me. When you were gone, and I thought that I might never see you again, I realized that I should have told you too."

Kami swallowed hard and squeezed his hand, staring into his eyes and wishing that she knew the words to say to convey her feelings. As it was, she felt tongue-tied and speechless.

He was a good man. He deserved so much from her, something other than an awkward attempt at sharing her muddled feelings.

Gabe slowly leaned closer to her, closing the distance between then in the tight confines of the sedan. His lips met hers in a sweet, tender kiss, his hands coming up to cup the back of her head gently and draw her closer.

She kissed him back tentatively, using the kiss as an outlet to convey the emotions that she was having difficulty saying aloud.

His kiss was undemanding, comforting even, and filled with such tender regard that Kami never wanted it to end. But when he brought the kiss to a slow close, tenderly sliding his lips from her mouth to lay a soft kiss on her cheek and drawing her close in the warm circle of his arms, Kami realized that was almost as good. She felt safe and protected in his embrace, perhaps even a little cherished. He made her feel good again, despite the events of the day. His embrace soothed her frayed emotions in a way that a hot bath and a nap never could. His touch burrowed its way into her heart and brought a warm there that has been missing for a long, long time.

She felt loved.

A sigh of contentment escaped her as she reveled in the moment.

The words that had felt so awkward only a moment ago now came easily to her lips, "I love you, Gabe."

His arms tightened around her for a moment, and his lips came back to hers. He kissed her gently again, just a quick brush of his lips over hers, and she felt his warm breath against her face as he whispered to her. "I love you, too, Kami. More than you can imagine."

He stroked her hair and drew her close again, and they sat that way, unmoving and silent, wrapped in strong emotion. Time seemed to stand still as they embraced, minutes ticking by as he held her tenderly.

103

She savored the moment, trying to just enjoy it and block out the events of the day, and all the questions that she had. All to quickly though, they intruded.

"What are we going to do now?" Kami asked softly, not sure herself whether she was referring to their newly formed relationship, or her other problems, or both.

"Marry me?" Gabe asked huskily.

She was taken by surprise. That was the last thing that she had expected him to say.

He drew back a little and looked into her face, "Before you answer, I want you to hear me out. I know it seems spur of the moment, and it is, but I believe that God has brought us together for a reason, Kami. It almost feels as if I am meant to protect you, to be with you, to love you. Do you feel that way too?"

She knew that her eyes must show her shock at his sudden proposal, but she nodded. She'd wondered the first day she'd met him if he was an answer to her prayers. At the time, she thought that he might be an answer to her prayer for help in the situation she found herself in, but now she realized that me might also have been the answer to the prayer she'd prayed so many times before. The prayer she'd prayed for a husband that she could build a family with. The one that she could live the rest of her life with.

"We don't have to get married this month, or even this year. We can have a long engagement if you want, but I needed for you to know my intentions. I want you to know that I want you for my wife," Gabe's voice was earnest as he made the admission.

Kami looked into his eyes and knew her

answer immediately. She'd been so lonely and closed-off since her grandfather's death. She'd wanted someone to share her life with, a man to build a family with. Someone to grow old with. Gabe, with his gentle compassion, easy-going nature, capable strength and firm faith in God was that man. She'd spent so many days in his company lately that it was hard to imagine not having him in her life now. He'd become so much more than just a protector to her.

Love for him squeezed her heart, but her words, when she spoke, were only a little breathless.

"Yes, Gabe, yes. I'll marry you. It does seem sudden, but I feel that bond with you too, as if our relationship is an answered prayer."

Gabe grinned at her, looking as if he'd just received a much-coveted gift. Then he enfolded her in his embrace once more.

After a moment, she felt his chest move against her cheek as he chuckled.

"We'd better go inside, I can see Jamie staring at us through the window. I'm surprised she hasn't come out here and dragged us both from the car already. I know that she was worried about you too."

Kami felt laughter bubble up inside of her at the thought of the super thin woman dragging Gabe anywhere. Her laughter replacing the emotional lump that had been lodged in her throat only a few moments before. With her heart overflowing with joy at Gabe's proposal, she suddenly saw the humor in the situation as well. He was right. From the very short time that she'd known Jamie, she could tell that the woman didn't have a lot of restraint. It was a wonder that she wasn't in the car with them, grilling them about their future plans and then trying to get the details of the accident out of them at the same time.

"Yes, we'd better," she gave him one last squeeze and drew back, not able to resist giving him a quick smooch on the lips one more time. Just knowing that he returned her feelings and that he was going to be her husband released a feeling inside her that she thought to never have. "I love you, Gabe."

"I love you too, Kami."

They shared another grin before sliding out of the car and entered the agency.

Jamie gave them an indecipherable look as they entered. Kami tried to wipe the grin off of her face, but she was having a hard time, especially in the face of such and expression of disgruntled joy.

"First, you're kidnapped, with your life hanging in the balance, and then you're in the parking lot kissing my boss. Kami, do you always lead such an eventful life?"

Kami couldn't help but laugh, "No, usually my life if boring and lonely, Jamie."

"Spill it, you two, I know something momentous happened, and I'm not talking about the kidnapping. I can see that Kami survived well enough. But, seeing you two getting all cozy out in the car really did surprise me."

Kami looked at Gabe, wondering if he was going to tell his friend the good news. When he just winked at her and smiled, she blurted out the news herself. "Gabe asked me to marry him. And I accepted."

She'd thought Gabe's friend would be happy for them, so Kami was surprised at Jamie's reaction. The woman looked a little disapproving.

Kami felt the smile fade from her face.

"Do you both think that's a good idea?" Jamie asked, looking between them both anxiously. "I mean, what just happened was an emotional roller coaster ride for both of you. You're both surely still under the influence of a bit of adrenaline at the very least. Do you think it is wise to be making life plans right now?"

Her eyes sought out Gabe's face, and Kami wondered whether to feel jealous of their close relationship that allowed the woman to speak so plainly, or offended that Jamie didn't seem to want her to marry her boss.

"Don't get me wrong, I think you two make a great couple. You're very compatible from what I've seen so far, it's just that this seems like a bit of a rush to me. I mean, seriously Gabe, did you even get her a ring before you proposed?"

Gabe looked as if he didn't know what to say in the face of Jamie's calm logic. His lips compressed slightly and his jaw worked a bit, "No, not yet, but I will. I know it seems sudden, Jamie, and I know that we're both still feeling the after-effects of Kami's brush with danger, but that's the whole point. It could have been too late, and I'd have never gotten to tell her how I feel about her. I want her to be my wife, and after the day's events, I want her to know that I want her to be my wife."

Jamie nodded, then looked at Kami, "And you? You don't think it is too sudden?"

Kami shook her head, "No, I'm glad to know how he feels because I feel the same way. It could have been too late, Jamie, don't you understand? I could have died, and..." her voice broke a little and she paused to gather her composure once more. "And I would have died without ever living my life. I've

107

been hiding behind a barrier, Jamie, but today I realized that I need to put that time behind me and just live my life, for however long I'm blessed with. I'd like to spend that time with Gabe."

Jamie nodded again, looking thoughtful. "I worry about you two, but you're right. We're only given one life to live and we should grab it with both hands."

"Besides," Kami felt as if she needed to explain further. "I think Gabe is an answer to my prayers, Jamie."

Jamie grinned, "Perhaps, and I'm not one to argue with the Big Guy, so I guess I'll just butt out now. Congratulations, you two. I hope I'm invited to the wedding?"

"Of course," Kami laughed. Jamie was Gabe's friend, and the woman who had helped to save her life today. Of course she was invited!

"So, let's get started on the will, shall we? The faster we wrap this up, the sooner you two can be on your way. Not to be horribly blunt, Kami, but despite the joy that becoming engaged has obviously given you, you really do look a little the worse for wear."

Kami nodded, not feeling at all self-conscious. "I must, because I am."

"This will be quick. I have a template for a living will that I downloaded from a lawyer's site. I talked to him earlier and he said to just email it to him when it's done. It's pretty short and to the point."

"Thank goodness for that!" Kami crossed the room and pulled up a chair beside Jamie's desk. "I'm ready to put this behind me. Let's just make it simple and put Gabe as the sole beneficiary."

Jamie's fingers typed quickly for several

minutes. "Okay, done. I'll print it out, you can sign it, I can sign as the witness, and since I also happen to be a notary, I can affix my seal. Then I'll just scan it and send it back to the lawyer."

"Thank you, Jamie, for making this all so easy on me."

"You're welcome, and you'll be glad to know that I typed up a press release about it too. By tomorrow, anyone who read the papers will know that you've made a will and left all the money to a non-disclosed beneficiary who just happens to *not* be your aunt or your uncle." Jamie chuckled a bit. "I'll bet that will rankle when it comes out in the papers, not that they don't deserve a nose-tweak like this if what we suspect is true."

"Oh, but it *is* true," Kami said, realizing belatedly that she had not filled Jamie in on the details that they'd learned at the police station. "After he was arrested, the guy who kidnapped me admitted everything. He gave a full written confession. It was my uncle who hired those men. And they were supposed to kill me, not kidnap me, but the man today decided that he wanted the money himself. He was planning to force me to marry him."

"Hmm, so there were wedding bells in your future no matter what, huh?" Jamie asked wryly, making a face.

Kami chuckled, "Yes, I guess there were. But I'd rather be able to choose my own groom. One who I actually *want* to spend the rest of my life with."

She looked at Gabe as she said the words, hoping that he could see the depth of her feeling for him in her eyes.

He smiled back at her, his own eyes filled with emotion. Then he winked and sauntered over to lean his hip against Jamie's desk, crossing his arms across his broad chest in a gesture of ease.

"Seems as if the guy who snatched Kami was eager to tell them everything he knew after he realized how much trouble he was in. He not only admitted to working for Kami's uncle, but he said that Kami's aunt had helped plan the thing too. He'd been contracted by them both to kill her, but he told police that he'd decided that if he was going to do the dirty work, he might as well get the money for himself, and he said that he had decided to kidnap Kami and keep her until she agreed to marry him. He also told them that several others had been hired to get the job done as well, and that was why things had escalated so quickly. They were in competition. The first one to finish the job was to get half a million dollars."

"It is hard to believe what greed will drive a person to do," Jamie shook her head, looking sad. "I still cannot wrap my head around the fact that Kami's own uncle would pay someone to kill his niece. Where has human decency gone in this society, Gabe?" Jamie shook her head again.

"So, completing the will is really just a formality," Gabe told her. "Since the police were planning on arresting her uncle as soon as they could locate him. But, when we shared our plans with the detective in charge, he thought it was a good idea to go ahead and get the will completed, just to cover all of our bases. The press release is a nice touch, Jamie."

"I thought you'd like that part. After it comes out in the paper the whole world will know that there's not a chance that Kami's aunt and uncle will ever get the money. Perhaps any stray hit men will get the message too. Especially after the arrests are made. Maybe your grandfather really did know what he was doing when he left it all to you, Kami?"

"Maybe he did. I never wanted to see the evil in my aunt and uncle. I always hoped for a reconciliation. But, there had to be a good reason why my grandfather cut them from his life so completely. I just wish I knew why my mother was estranged from him as well." Kami shook her head. "I guess I'll never know now."

"Maybe it's better not knowing?" Jamie suggested.

"Maybe you're right." Kami agreed.

Chapter Fifteen

The room was an upheaval of chaos, with tiny white-clad flower girls running about the room and their mothers trying to corral them and talk them into behaving with dignity. Of course, it was hard to behave with dignity when one was only five years old, which seemed to be the median age of the four flower girls who were doing the honors at Kami's wedding.

The ladies of the church had come together in a big way to help Kami plan the wedding. She'd decided that God's will was God's will, and waiting a year to get married wouldn't change how she felt about Gabe or the fact that he was a blessing inserted into her life. With the close brush with death had come the desire to live her life fully and so, following that tenet, she had managed to organize the wedding in only four days. The trip to Hawaii would serve as their honeymoon.

It hadn't been easy to plan a wedding in only for days, especially since Gabe had insisted on going through pre-marriage counseling with the minister before the ceremony, but Kami once again had found that money opened doors that were normally very hard to open.

As she stood in the ladies prayer room of the church, clad in her wedding gown and surrounded by flowers, women and little girls, she looked at her face in the mirror and realized that she felt true happiness for perhaps the first time in her adult life.

She closed her eyes amidst the chaos of the room and quickly gave thanks to the Lord for his blessings, and for bringing Gabe into her life.

As promised in his Word, He had been faithful in a time of tribulation, and had made all things – even attempted kidnapping and multiple contracts on her life – turn out for her good. *For the good of those who love him…*

"Taking a moment of silence before hitching yourself to my boss?" Jamie asked at her elbow.

"No, just thanking God for Gabe. He's perfect."

Jamie nodded, "Don't let him hear you say that, although it is true. Gabe is a great guy, but we should try to keep him at least a little humble."

Jamie winked at her, then gave her a quick hug just as the first strains of the Wedding March began to play, signaling the beginning to the start of her new life.

If you enjoyed *Guarding Kami*, please consider leaving a review of the book on Amazon. I would love to know what you thought of the story, and even if you have suggestions about upcoming books.

If you'd like to receive updates about new releases, contests, free copies, and subscriber-only specials, please sign up for my newsletter at: www.janeanworth.com

Other books by Janean Worth:

Mind Mods Series – Young Adult Sci-Fi
Mind Mods (now FREE on Amazon)
Infected
Brain Bots
Mind Mods Bundle (get all three books bundled together for a discounted price)

Sam Stone Series – Romantic Suspense
Deep Down

Narrow Gate Series – Teen Christian Dystopian
After the Fall (now FREE on Amazon)
The Narrow Gate

Excerpt of **Deep Down** – a new Romantic Suspense
novel by Janean Worth

Prologue

Hugo Mack discarded the miner's coveralls he'd donned while posing as an employee of the Sareyville Salt Company, broke open the sterile packaging containing the auto-injector pen that he'd been given and then unceremoniously stabbed himself in the leg with it, injecting the contents into the bulky muscles in his right thigh. The serum burned through his leg like fire, entering his blood stream quickly and burning along his veins all the way to his brain. He drew in a gasping wheeze in surprise at the severity of the pain. He hadn't expected it to burn. His employer had told him nothing about that unpleasant side effect. Hugo breathed deeply and the burning sensation quickly passed, leaving behind only a pleasantly warm tingle that stretched throughout his entire body, chasing away the slight chill in the air that came from being deep under ground.

A little irritated that his employer hadn't cautioned him about the burning fire that had spread through his body so quickly, Hugo made a mental note to raise the price of the job slightly as compensation for the serum's initial unpleasantness. He'd agreed to kill people, not become a lab rat himself. A little danger came with every job, and for this one in particular, but Hugo didn't like needles, and he didn't particularly like his employer either, so he felt justified in demanding a few extra thousand for his troubles.

Hugo dug in his pocket and pulled out his cell phone then activated the stopwatch feature, avidly watching the softly glowing screen in the surrounding darkness as it counted up to two minutes. The

117

instructions had been clear. He must wait two full minutes after injecting himself with the serum before completing his next task. Otherwise, the serum would not protect him from the toxic substance that he was about to unleash.

The stopwatch app passed the two-minute mark, but Hugo waited another full minute before closing the app and pocketing his phone, just to be safe.

Before approached the bank of metal lockers that stood before him in the dark cavern that had been carved from salt and rock, he grabbed the thick, rubber-coated gloves that his employer had provided him with, donned the protective rubber apron and plastic face shield that had come with the gloves, and then snatched up his own large claw-foot hammer that he'd brought along from his garage. He had used guns on his jobs before, many times. A few times he'd used a knife. But, he'd never been hired to kill people using a hammer before. The thought made him chuckle quietly in the dark.

Before he began, he adjusted the miner's light upon his forehead, taking care to avoid the new, fresh tattoo that ran in thick black lines from his hairline to his jaw along the left side of his face. He'd gotten the tattoo to celebrate the job he was doing now. When it was complete, he'd have hit a new record. He'd have over two hundred kills under his belt. The new tattoo represented the completion of a long-term goal.

He positioned the light so that it shone exactly straight ahead of him into the gloom, smirking again a little as he did so. He'd never thought he'd *ever* have occasion to wear a miner's light. He idly wondered if any other hit man in the history of the world had ever had to use a miner's light during the course of a job before. He shrugged at the fanciful thought. *Probably not.*

Stepping forward, he pried open the metal front panel of the locker labeled C-1249 with the claw on the hammer. Inside, as promised, the space was filled with ten neatly stacked cylindrical aluminum containers, all precisely labeled with brightly colored decals proclaiming the toxic nature of their contents. The cylinders were almost completely covered with images of skulls with crossbones, bright yellow hazard triangles and large red 'DANGER' ovals.

Hugo ignored the warning decals and raised the claw-footed hammer over the nearest cylinder. Then he paused, wondering… Would the serum provided by his employer truly protect him from the toxic mess he was about to release?   Did he trust the man that much?

The hammer grew heavy in his hand as he contemplated the answer. No, he didn't trust the man with his life, but Hugo *had* been very clear what would happen if he should happen to die down in the mines with the others. So, he may not trust the *man*, but he *did* trust that his employer would do anything to ensure that Hugo's failsafe, his package of dirty secrets that had been obtained before Hugo had accepted the job, would remain hidden. The damning evidence of those secrets, photos and photocopied images of hidden documents, had been loaded into a program and set on a schedule that would disseminate the information digitally across a host of social media websites if Hugo didn't return in time to cancel the uploads. If Hugo were to die unexpectedly that night, or in the following forty-eight hours, his employer's secrets would be exposed for the world to see.   Hugo knew that his employer would never do to anything to jeopardize his own good standing, so keeping Hugo safe had become a priority as soon as Hugo had told the man about the files.

Reassured now of his own safety, Hugo raised the hammer a little higher and then brought it down hard on the flanged collar of the cylinder, smashing into the soft aluminum with powerful force. The canister depressurized with a soft hiss as the metal bent and buckled. Hugo used the hammer's claw to pry open the top a bit more so that the thick black sludge inside could ooze out as he tipped the canister onto its side.

He quickly repeated the process with the other nine canisters, giving only a fleeting thought to the hundred or so innocent people that would die that night because of his actions. When he was done, he stepped back and tossed the blackened hammer aside. He ripped the annoying rubber apron from his chest and then quickly divested himself of the remaining protective gear, throwing the black-spattered plastic and rubber on top of the discarded hammer.

Smiling in satisfaction, he turned away from the quickly spreading oozing black sludge and strode out of the darkened cavern, his miner's light bobbing brightly with every step, happy with the knowledge that he'd just earned himself a cool half million dollars.

Corporate espionage, with a large side of murder, certainly paid well.

Chapter One

Jenny Strafford tried to calm her racing heart, but it pounded in her throat like the beat of a drum. She reminded herself several times that this was supposed to be a fun outing – a double date with two of her fiancé's friends and their family.

The friends, Gilbert and Debbie, had called her fiancé the day before, offering a rare chance at a spot for a dinner theater, held in the underground salt museum in their hometown of Hawkington, Kansas. Jenny had never met either of them, but her fiancé had insisted that the offer of an outing had been too good to pass up, since most of the dinner theater performances were only for select patrons of the museum.

That was how Jenny now found herself in the museum's modest waiting room, a hard hat clutched in her sweating fingers, awaiting their group's turn to ride the powered lift down to the museum, which resided 640 feet below ground level in an area of tunnels that had been excavated and used as a working salt mine until just recently when it had been partially converted into the museum.

Jenny shivered in cold dread and reached out to grasp her fiancé's warm fingers, wondering what had possibly possessed her to agree to this outing. She did not like enclosed spaces, or the thought of being trapped and unable to exit any place when she wished. By going deep underground in the lift, she was effectively trapping herself underground until the museum's lift operator could bring her back to the surface. And the lifts ran only at scheduled times, worked by the experienced operator to avoid death or injury to the occupants of the lift - or so the tour guide had said during the mandatory safety lecture that they'd all attended.

Entrusting her very life into the hands of a stranger was not something that Jenny did easily. Without her fiancé's comforting presence at her side, she would never have even considered it. But, the outing had seemed to represent an adventure to him, and she didn't want to disappoint him, knowing that he wouldn't attend without her. Besides, she'd just finished her latest project, a glossy photo book detailing the intricate work of handcrafting wire jewelry, and she was ready to begin another book project in the next month or so. Perhaps a visit to the underground salt museum would provide a bit of inspiration?

It had been two long weeks since she and her fiancé, Stone, had been able to spend any significant time together. Their last 'date' had been a week-long trip to Fort Lauderdale, Florida. It had been a wonderful vacation, and they'd both soaked up the sun, enjoyed fishing, surfing and lying on the beach together, and in general, just had the time of their lives. But, since then, they'd seen very little of each other. Stone's new job running his own security consultant business had been requiring him to be out of town often now, and she'd let the rote of daily life and the deadline to finish the book consume her schedule. Jenny knew that it would do them both good to go out with friends, wishing only that the dinner theater had been held above ground.

Stone squeezed her fingers reassuringly, then reached over to take the hard hat from the shaking fingers of her other hand. He perched it upon her head and squashed it down over her riot of dark curls, grinning at what she was sure was a very ridiculous look for her. Hard hats were *not* her style, but the tour guide had insisted that each visitor must wear one at all times while underground, citing various rules and regulation. Personally, Jenny thought this was a foolish and silly rule. A hard hat was not going to protect her if the mine caved in. Nothing would, short of a miracle. At the thought, another shiver of dread skated up her spine.

If Jenny were truthful, she remembered little of the list of rules that the guide had spouted, since at the time of the instruction, her mind had been caught up in a litany of fear and dread, much as it was now as they waited for their turn on the lift.

"It'll be *fine,*" Stone said, giving her a wink. "You'll see. You'll have fun."

Jenny smiled brightly at him, ignoring the dread that pooled in her stomach, "Sure, can't wait."

By the look on his face, Stone knew that she was lying, but he said nothing, just giving her another grin. He was always telling her that she was a terrible liar, and that anyone could read the expression on her face and immediately know what she was thinking. At that moment, Jenny hoped it wasn't true, because that would mean that both Gilbert and Debbie, was well as Stone and the other visitors clustered around them, would all know that she was utterly terrified.

Jenny swallowed hard, focusing on Stone's beautiful brown eyes and the strength of his fingers as he took her hand again.

You can do this! she coached herself, but she doubted even her own inner voice. This seemed to be a very bad idea, and she couldn't seem to convince herself that it wasn't.

As the lift operator called out the number of their group, letting them know that their turn was next, Jenny took a long breath and then patted her pocket, assuring herself that her inhaler was there, safe and sound, and within easy reach to rescue her should she have an asthma attack while down in the mines.

Satisfied that the inhaler was there, she then thought longingly of her other source of protection, the .38 revolver that she'd been forced to leave in the locked box in her vehicle. She hadn't been out of the house without the revolver concealed inside her clothing in more than a year – ever since she'd gotten her concealed carry permit at Stone's insistence after she'd been the victim of a close-call attack. Museum rules did not permit concealed weapons of any type, so Jenny had been forced to leave the gun behind, and now she felt almost naked without it.

She gripped Stone's hand tighter, comforting herself with the thought that the tour guide had informed them of the presence of no less than five armed security guards down in the museum below. Apparently, the dinner theater performance was going to be attended by a celebrity of some renown, who's identity had not yet been revealed to the other museum patrons, and additional security had been provided for the night's entertainment to provide added protection for the unnamed individual.

Reminding herself once more that this was supposed to be a *fun* outing, Jenny took a deep breath, pasted a smile on her face and followed the others into the lift, listening as the iron door closed with a clank behind her, sealing them all into the small dark area.

No one had warned her that the ride down would be conducted in total darkness, and Jenny shivered in dread as the lift plummeted quickly through the blackness, taking her farther underground that she'd ever wished to venture.

For a moment, she cursed her people-pleasing tendencies – knowing she'd only agreed to accompany Stone because she'd wanted to make him happy. Gulping back fear, she began to count the minutes until she could return to top of the lift. Already, the air had begun to feel a bit stagnant, and they'd only just begun the ride down. Pressure gathered in her ears and pressed upon her chest. Reflexively, her fingers sought the shape of the inhaler through the faded denim of her jeans.

Chapter Two

The lift was surprisingly fast, and Jenny felt the metal compartment descend the full 640 feet underground in a blindingly fast blur. Her ears popped once on the way down, but the complete darkness hid the features of the other visitors, so she could not tell if any of them experienced the same feeling of fleeting discomfort.

In moments, they were escaping the double-decker lift, and Jenny exited the iron compartment gratefully, stepping out into a softly glimmering world of caverns and tunnels sparkling with salt. The mines looked nothing like she'd thought they would. Everywhere, the chiseled walls and carved out ceiling of the tunnels glittered with billions of sparkling crystals, glittering in the dim light cast by rows of lights mounted onto the ceiling. Motes of sparkling salt dust, stirred up by the motion of the lift, danced in the air, contributing to the otherworldly beauty even as it clogged the airways and nasal passages of the visitors. Even the air was different in the caverns, brackish and odd smelling, having a thick quality that immediately made Jenny's asthmatic lungs tighten in reaction. The air seemed strange and slightly abnormal, redolent with the smell of dirt and salt, with an odd undertone that wasn't particularly pleasant. The undertone scent was acidic, with a slight chemical edge. No one else seemed to notice the odd quality to the air, or if they did notice, they didn't seem to be bothered by it. Jenny thought that perhaps, once again, she was just being too sensitive to her environment.

Despite her apprehension of being so far underground, and the strange quality of the air, Jenny found the softly glimmering, shimmering space oddly beautiful.

"Welcome to the Strata underground museum," another perky, cheerful female tour guide announced as the remaining visitors exited the lift, pushing out behind Jenny and Stone like a small stampede, blinking like owls suddenly thrust into the light. "You have about thirty minutes before the dinner theater portion of tonight's entertainment begins, so please, if you wish, take that time to look at the museum's exhibits and gift shop before you find your assigned table. There will also be an intermission later, at which time you're welcome to resume your exploration of the museum portion of the mines. Please, do *not* wander away from the museum area for any reason during the evening's festivities. And, always remember to wear your hard hat."

The blonde tour guide gave them all a megawatt smile, full of skillfully whitened, precisely straight teeth, and then gestured for them to begin their exploration of the museum.

Jenny looked off down the excavated tunnels that bisected the main area of the museum, and wondered why anyone would even contemplate wandering off from the group into the dark recesses of the mine. She shuddered at the thought of missing her ride back to the surface. Surely only a certifiably *insane* person would wander off and chance being stuck down in the mines for an extended period of time?

Stone felt her shiver and smiled at her reassuringly. "Come on, let's go see the exhibits."

"Debbie and I have seen the exhibits several times on our previous visits here, so I'll go find our table while you two look around. We'll meet you in the dining area in twenty," Gilbert said, taking Debbie's hand and leading her off down the wide tunnel. They strode past the antique mining equipment and huge salt boulders that were on display, lining the sides of the tunnel, and headed off toward the dining area where the dinner theater would be performed.

Debbie's twenty-something niece, Alice, and Debbie's elderly mother and father, Paul and Cheryl, who had joined their small group for the evening's entertainment, followed after the couple, leaving Jenny alone with Stone in the dimly sparkling entry cavern.

Jenny tried not to cough as their departing footsteps stirred up tiny puffs of salt-laden dust from the floor of the mine, knowing that coughing would only exacerbate the feeling of tightness in her lungs. She hoped that the next few hours passed quickly, because she was already anticipating taking a huge breath of fresh air when they returned to the surface again.

"Here, would you carry this for a bit? It's getting heavy," Jenny said as she slid her heavy backpack-style purse off of her shoulder and handed it to Stone.

Stone took the bag from her and effortlessly slung the strap over his shoulder. "What have you got in this thing, Jenny? It is more than a little heavy, especially for you to be carrying around down here for hours."

"Oh, you know, a little of this, a little of that. Healthy snacks in case I don't like dinner, a couple of extra bottles of water for us in case we get thirsty, aspirin, lip balm. That kind of thing. You know I like to be prepared."

Stone chuckled, but said nothing, reaching over to take her hand again.

Pulling her Droid from her pocket one-handed as Stone held her other hand, Jenny snapped a few photos of the enormous, deeply veined and marbled salt boulder directly in front of them, intending to send them out via Snapchat. She groaned softly when she remembered that there would be no cellular service so far underground. Since she normally spent so much time on her phone, texting and making calls, this lack of service disturbed her greatly, and she felt even more cut off from world than she had just a moment before as they'd stepped off of the lift. No calls, no texting, no Instagram or Snapchat, no Facebook or Twitter – no sort of outside connection for the next four hours.

This dinner theater had better be spectacular, she thought.

With a small sigh, she crammed her now almost useless cell phone into her pocket and followed Stone's tug on her hand as he led them further into the mines. She'd be glad when this 'fun' was over and she could leave behind the mildly panicky feeling of being underground, where, to her logical writer's mind, it made absolutely no sense for any intelligent human to be willing to venture.

DEEP DOWN is available in ebook format on Amazon and in paperback wherever fine books are sold.

44160604R00082

Made in the USA
Charleston, SC
16 July 2015